Jalby

and the

Brain Programmers

Mark L. Turner

For mum and dad

With thanks to Beth for reading the manuscript and for her encouragement.

Chapter 1

Jalby looked at the vast bank of digital displays and started to wonder if it was all a terrible mistake. The boy was strapped to the bed in the operating theatre and couldn't move a muscle. What if the scientists made a mistake? Would his brain be pulverised?

He was wearing a large helmet which was connected to a formidable looking machine – a fifty petaflop supercomputer more powerful even than the computer which controlled the Mars landing back in 2055.

The displays all showed zero and the computer was humming away quietly, but Jalby felt uneasy – any second now thousands of electrical impulses would be sent through the helmet and into his brain.

He watched as the two scientists scurried around.

The chief scientist, Professor Meribrayne, stopped and peered at the machine. She was a large woman who always seemed to wear the same ill-fitting lab coat. Nothing mattered to her, apart from her work. Sometimes she even forgot to go home at night, as she obsessed over every detail of the project.

She was talking hurriedly to her assistant, Doctor Scorpface, a small, nervous looking man who was darting around checking equipment.

Jalby tried to listen in, but could only catch snippets of what Professor Meribrayne was saying.

'Let's increase the voltage by 20 volts.'

He didn't like the sound of this. Wasn't the voltage already set high enough?

'We'll see how he responds after the first few minutes,' Meribrayne continued.

Jalby had been led to believe that the procedure would only last three minutes. He had been lying there, fully conscious, for two hours and he was starting to get agitated. Still, he was hoping he would never again have to memorise tiresome dates in history class, or remember how a common toad breathes in tedious biology lessons. Just then, Scorpface raised his voice. 'The pulse generator is behaving strangely. Have you ever seen it do that before?' he asked Meribrayne.

'Shush, don't alarm the boy,' she whispered; although it was easily loud enough for Jalby to hear. Scorpface was gawping at a display that resembled the Himalayas, but everything seemed under control again a few seconds later.

'It's settled down again – we're nearly there,' Meribrayne said

8

finally.

Jalby wondered if he could stop the operation. A small croak escaped from his throat, unheard or ignored by the scientists. His pulse was quickening and beads of sweat were starting to form on his forehead. 'Ok, the infoscanner is ready Scorpface. We just need to tweak his neurons a little with a few impulses.'

Scorpface flicked some switches, but then made a stupid mistake.

'No, not that much – reduce the frequency!' Meribrayne exploded.

Even though Jalby was the last to be hooked up to the computer, they still seemed scarily incompetent.

'Good. That's better,' she said more calmly.

Just as Jalby was starting to feel they had actually forgotten there was a real, live human wired up to their contraption, Meribrayne came over to speak to him.

'We're all set now. Feeling OK?'

Jalby attempted to look as confident as possible, as he tried to nod. He remembered the vice-like grip of the clasp around his head.

'Yes,' he mumbled.

'Don't worry,' Meribrayne tried to reassure him. 'The procedure is very quick, and quite painless.'

He wondered how she could say that when clearly she had never undergone the process.

It was useless for adults anyway – the procedure could only work on children, because their brains were still developing so quickly. Adults were too old, so it was up to children like Jalby to test the scientists' ideas.

Jalby was tall and mature for his age, and his teachers thought he would be a good candidate for Meribrayne's work. He had been top of the class a few years before, but recently his work had been going from bad to worse. It was their last attempt to improve his dismal school marks.

He remembered what he had been told. For the technique to work, he had to clear his head of any negative thoughts. He almost wished he had been to a meditation class, but meditation didn't seem the done thing when you were Jalby's age.

Just then, Jalby felt the first of the impulses – small signals sent to stimulate his brain, before the real procedure began. A strange, fuzzy feeling enveloped his head and he had to fight to keep calm. What was it he had been told? On no account must he panic. Just what would happen if he did, no one would tell him. He had the impression it would not be pretty. He had visions of his brain quickly boiling, and grey matter exploding across the laboratory and the scientists' white coats.

'OK, I think that's enough,' Meribrayne murmured. 'Let's start the high energy impulses.'

When the impulses spread through his brain, it was as if a star had blown up inside his head. He felt as if the connections between his brain cells were being ripped apart – thousands of them every second. All his senses were suddenly on alert. A few seconds later and he could taste every type of food he had ever tried, one after the other, each one lasting just a fraction of a second. What was that one? Rhubarb crumble, followed by boiled cabbage, and then custard! There was no sense to his senses. There were even flavours he had never tasted in his life, including one he imagined might be fried spiders, and another one, pickled monkey brain.

He almost panicked when he felt something hairy brush against his arm, and then something was breathing in his face, when all he could see was a sunflower swaying in the breeze. A moment later he was looking at a nice country house with chimpanzees swinging from the trees, while he could smell chicken curry. It was like a particularly weird dream.

Suddenly there was an ear piercing scream and he was plunged underwater, the scream still ringing in his ears. He felt himself struggling for breath and then noticed a dark shape moving quickly towards him. He tried to get away, but his legs felt like they were embedded in cement, dragging him to the bottom. The shape took on the form of a creature he had never seen in his life. Perhaps it was one of those genetically mutated monster fish people had seen swimming in the Thames. Whatever it was, it was ugly. It was thrusting its jaws out ready to catch Jalby round the middle. He could see its razor-sharp teeth, about to rip into him, and then, amazingly, it took on the form of his aunt.

The sterile surroundings of the lab drifted back into view, a little hazy at first, and Jalby could see the two scientists looking down at him. Meribrayne was beaming.

'That was just something to open up your senses for the next phase,' she said, obviously quite pleased with herself. 'I hope your mind didn't treat you too badly! No doubt you experienced many things – but they were just illusions.'

Just illusions, thought Jalby. He was in a cold sweat. He hadn't realised his mind was capable of such things.

'Now we come to the reason we're all here – brain programming,' Meribrayne announced.

He remembered something he had been told before they wheeled him into the operating theatre – once they had opened up his senses, there was no going back. Jalby's brain, in this state, would never be able to learn anything properly ever again – unless he carried on with the procedure. He had to go on with the programming, or he would probably spend the rest of his days struggling with basic algebra. He could see himself now – fifty years old and in a class of 12-year-olds laughing at him as he failed to answer yet another question. He didn't get the impression the scientists had considered this. To them, their research was a work of art. They thought nothing could possibly go wrong with the technique they had spent twenty years devising.

Jalby cleared his mind. At least the next phase wasn't supposed to be as unpredictable. He had had a unique microchip implanted deep into his brain, which would help him to store all the knowledge he would ever need. The school subjects Jalby had slaved over were going to be programmed into his brain effortlessly. All he had to do was just lie back and think of nothing. What could be easier? Even better, he would never have to revise for exams, because the microchip would create a permanent memory for each subject – he would never forget any of it.

Jalby could feel the excitement rising in him. He would show them all how he could return to form. He only wished the machine would also program his favourite music into his brain. He had had a tiny voice-controlled stereo embedded in his ears a few years before, like the rest of his friends. Whenever he downloaded music to it, the cost was automatically deducted from his pocket money.

Scorpface was now behind a huge console while Meribrayne was staring at a dozen different screens, all showing vast amounts of information.

'Ok Scorpface. It's time. Let's crank it up.'

Somehow Jalby expected more technical language from the country's top brain scientist, but surely she knew what she was doing.

A high-pitched whirring sound came from the machine as the microprocessor kicked into action. Not even the ancient computers at school made this sort of noise, thought Jalby.

'Start the infoscanner,' Meribrayne ordered.

Jalby braced himself as Scorpface punched several codes onto a screen. A few seconds later and the machine started to howl, drowning out anything the scientists said.

The first subject, Jalby had been told, would be geography. Hardly his favourite. He had been trying to grasp the finer points of the Earth's catastrophic problems for months.

He waited, trying to imagine how it was going to feel to have thousands of facts stamped into his mind every second. He didn't have to wait long. There was a sudden flash before his eyes, and then it began. They were like a flicker of disjointed movie images, one after the other, forced into his brain. Areas of London now under the sea, Greenland almost melted, rainforest decimated –

replaced with hover scooter racecourses and giant theme parks showing what life was like before the environment was wrecked. At least England was green – greener than it had ever been. Whenever anyone went on a space plane, they always planted a tree, so they wouldn't feel so guilty about all the pollution they had just caused. People now came to London to see what they thought was a rainforest with a city built in the middle of it.

There were also the facts – endless streams of data and numbers, so fast Jalby could only fix his attention on a few of them. Now, in the year 2060, the population of London was twenty million. The temperature in September often reached more than 30 degrees – England seemed almost tropical at times, apart from the freak snow storms that came out of nowhere. The government had tried to control the weather but gave up after killing every plant in the city in a heatwave.

What Jalby assumed were the main ideas of the subject seemed to form like a jigsaw in his mind, everything slotting into place amazingly quickly. It was like being in a hundred geography lessons all at once, except that they were actually enjoyable. Sometimes the programming left him with a vague impression, which he assumed was some half-baked theory, uploaded when no one really knew what was going on in the world.

Suddenly his brain started to hurt. It was overheating. He cursed himself. He was supposed to relax and let all the knowledge wash

15

over him – exactly the opposite of what he was supposed to be doing in class. The pain was starting to get unbearable. His head had never ached like this. He desperately tried to ignore the images by focusing on the ceiling. Then the data finally stopped. Jalby hardly dared to breathe. That was the end of geography.

He would have been happy, but he realised he had a lot more to go – all the other subjects: maths, science, English, Chinese, plus subjects he had not even studied yet.

His head was starting to feel cooler again as the whining of the processor built up to a piercing scream. Meribrayne came over to see if he was alright. Jalby wanted to tell her to wait, just another minute, but his head was spinning and his parched throat couldn't be made to speak. Meribrayne turned and nodded to Scorpface and Jalby braced himself for another onslaught.

It was maths. In fact Jalby quite enjoyed maths, unlike most of the children at school. It made sense and it was logical – usually. He felt like saying this wasn't necessary, that he could quite happily learn all he needed to know about maths, the old-fashioned way. Out of nowhere, numbers and equations flew into his mind. At first it wasn't so visual, but then graphs and charts and different shapes all flooded in.

He seemed to be getting better at this. His brain wasn't overheating anymore. He managed to look through the stream of figures and keep his mind clear. Once again the whining died down and maths was finished with.

The subjects seemed to follow more quickly now – English, art, science – but it was during the Chinese programming that it happened. Jalby was lying there, feeling very pleased that he would never have to learn another Chinese character. He realised his mind was drifting. 'Clear your thoughts,' he said to himself. Suddenly Jalby thought he heard Scorpface shout above the whine of the machine. There was an awful sound. Like the sound a brain might make if it was sucked through a straw. It didn't seem to come from Jalby. At least he didn't think it did. Out the corner of his eye he saw Meribrayne leap over to the console and start pushing frantically at the screen. It did not look very scientific. Then the whining intensified. This time it was like the sound of a very old jet engine – one that might just decide it had had enough. Jalby started to panic. What was going on? He saw the fear, the despair in the eyes of the scientists. There was an explosion. Jalby was blinded by an intense white flash, and then everything was black. He was slipping into unconsciousness. Then there was nothing.

Chapter 2

Jalby woke up feeling as if his brain had been sawn in two and sewn back together again, with very untidy stitches. He didn't feel as if he knew any more than he did before. There was just a stabbing pain all over his head, reminding him of his continued existence.

After a few seconds his head cleared and a blurred image of sterile white walls swam into view. He turned his head as gently as he could and a young nurse hurried over to see how he was.

'Take it easy,' she said softly. 'You'll be in some pain for a few days.'

'How long have I been unconscious?' Jalby managed to ask in a slurred voice.

'The accident happened two days ago,' the nurse replied. 'We were worried you might not pull through. At first the scientists thought the machine had damaged your brain when it blew up.'

'Will I be ok?'

'We think so, yes. You've come through it amazingly well. But we need to keep you here until all the signs are normal.'

'I feel like someone's had a go at my head with a machete,' Jalby moaned.

He suddenly realised he didn't know what had happened to Meribrayne or Scorpface. Perhaps he didn't actually care what had happened to them – they had almost finished him off with their crazy contraption.

'How are the scientists?' he found himself asking.

'Meribrayne is fine - she got behind the screen just in time.'

'And Scorpface?'

'They're still removing pieces of the brain programmer from his leg.'

Jalby had nasty visions of Scorpface wincing in pain as shrapnel and shards of glass were removed with a pair of tweezers. Perhaps he would test the next machine properly, before almost killing someone with it, he thought.

The nurse scuttled off, leaving Jalby to lie there, motionless. It was less painful if he didn't do anything.

He was just closing his eyes when Meribrayne walked into the ward. She was unscathed and looked remarkably relaxed, as if she was used to her inventions going badly wrong every day.

'Ah, my dear Jalby!' she said warmly as she approached the bed.

'Good to see you're awake. The doctor told me you'll be out of here soon.'

Jalby couldn't quite share her enthusiasm. He managed a weak smile as he tried to focus on her face.

'I'm so sorry about what happened in there,' she continued. 'We'd never had any problems with the machine until it was your turn.'

She made Jalby feel like he had somehow jinxed the programming.

'Sorry to throw a spanner in the works. What caused it?' he asked.

'We can't say yet. There seemed to be a surge in current through the circuits, and we couldn't, um, control it.'

Jalby rolled his eyes. 'That's an understatement,' he muttered. 'Will the machine work again?' he asked.

Meribrayne knocked over a vase of flowers as she turned to sit down on the chair next to Jalby's bed. She didn't seem to notice.

'Sadly, no,' she answered. 'We need to rebuild it from scratch and thoroughly test it before we allow anyone else near it.'

'So it wasn't tested properly?'

'Well, I wouldn't say that,' Meribrayne said cautiously. 'You can never be sure there won't be a few teething problems with new technology.'

Jalby felt pretty sure he wouldn't be volunteering next time.

'The good news,' Meribrayne went on, 'is that we have no reason to see why you shouldn't have an excellent grasp of all the subjects we programmed you with.'

'Do I have all the school subjects now, even Chinese?' Jalby asked eagerly.

'Yes. Well, almost.' Meribrayne seemed thoughtful for a moment. 'Perhaps you're not quite there with the Chinese yet. The little accident happened when we were nearly at the end of your Chinese lessons. You may notice a few small problems when you come to speak it.'

Jalby wasn't really thinking of going to China. Just as long as he left the hospital by the weekend and didn't have to go back to school, he would be quite happy.

'Will I really never need to go to school again?'

'Well, you'll just need to go once more with the other children we programmed. You all need to go to school again so you can be tested.'

Jalby had really started to dislike the word 'test'.

'You can't expect never to have lessons again, unless you're tested,' said Meribrayne firmly. 'But don't worry. You'll be tested with the ordinary school students, and their marks won't even come close. All of you will do brilliantly,' she said with a gleam in her eye.

Jalby lived in a commuter town on the outskirts of London, and his school had come bottom in the league table for the eighth year running. Meribrayne thought the lessons weren't up to much – that was why she had decided to put her research to the test at the school. She had only been allowed to try the programming on five children, but it was her mission to prove to the school, the parents and everyone else, that the technique was a work of genius. More than a few people seemed to think the scientist was out of her mind, but this just made her even more determined.

'So when will we be tested?' Jalby asked.

'Next week.'

Jalby couldn't help groaning.

'As the nurse said, you'll be fine. And don't forget, don't bother revising for your tests – you won't need to!'

Jalby had no intention of revising anything. He intended to stay in bed as long as possible.

22

'I'm expecting great things of you all,' Meribrayne said proudly. 'However, as soon as you've got your results, I'd like you to come back here, just for a quick check-up.'

'Just me?'

'Yes, just you. A precautionary measure, because of your accident with the programmer. It would be a good time to check everything's in order.'

Jalby was worried.

'Just a precaution,' Meribrayne repeated.

She gave him a last smile, got up and strode from the ward.

Jalby lay there thinking. He still felt as if someone was working away on his head with an axe. The room was still spinning, and the picture on the wall seemed to show dolphins leaping from the sea one second, and fat worms crawling from the ground the next. Worst of all, he still felt no signs of any great knowledge in his brain.

Perhaps Meribrayne was wrong. Perhaps he hadn't acquired any new knowledge at all. Maybe the accident had actually destroyed all memory of what little he had learned at school. He could soon be the laughing stock of the whole place.

To take his mind off the test, he ordered the TV at the end of his bed to turn on. It was the news. The newscaster had the usual overly serious tone to his voice. 'There are police reports concerning a child who went missing from a south coast village a month ago. The boy was discovered this morning, wandering along cliffs near the town of Shingleton. The boy seemed lost and has no memory of where he has been for the past month, or of how he came to be missing. He is now in hospital undergoing checks, but he appears unharmed. Anyone with any information is asked to contact the police.'

Jalby lost interest in the news after that. Just the usual squabbles between the political parties, and then a report on Martian Moggy – the first cat to be taken to Mars.

He told the TV to turn off and wondered if anyone would come to visit him. He couldn't stop thinking of the tests. He was dreading the next week.

Chapter 3

Jalby was being interrogated by his fearsome aunt, Malinka Malis, a small wiry woman who could terrorise anyone with her explosive temper. She was clearly sceptical of the idea of brain-programming.

'I'll believe it when I see it. I told you it was suspicious – them only being allowed to program five children,' she was barking as she stormed round the kitchen.

She checked on the progress of a large genetically modified house plant growing in the corner. It had several red and yellow fruits growing on it. The red ones tasted exactly like a steak – Jalby's favourite – but the yellow ones were revolting and smelled of fish that was past its use-by date. Malinka normally gave Jalby the yellow ones for dinner, saying that they were healthier.

'There's no substitute for a proper education,' she continued. 'No getting out of doing some hard work.'

She still thought that children should learn to write the old-fashioned way, when no one had actually used a pen and paper for years.

A few nights ago, she had picked Jalby up from the hospital.

She had been fussing over him as if he was six, embarrassing him in front of the nurse. 'Don't forget your computer,' she had nagged, 'and your phone.'

Now, back in the kitchen, Jalby didn't need reminding that the programming could have been a disaster.

'You young people always think there's an easy way out of doing things. Well, perhaps today you'll realise those scientists just used you as a guinea pig. I don't know what your uncle was thinking, sending you off to be programmed. I've told the school authorities to investigate this brain programming further. I don't think they knew what they were doing, allowing you to be programmed.'

Jalby had the impression his aunt secretly wanted the programming to fail so she would be proved right. After the machine had exploded though, he could hardly blame her for thinking the scientists were incompetent.

It was Jalby's uncle, Balton, who had wanted the boy to try the procedure. In the end, Malinka reluctantly agreed after seeing his exam results get even worse.

Jalby's school work had been suffering ever since his parents had mysteriously disappeared, two years before. They had said goodbye as he had jumped on his scooter and gone off to school. It was a normal day. He had come home and waited for them to get back from work. They had never returned. No one had heard anything from them – they had simply vanished without trace. The hardest thing was not knowing what had happened to them – not even knowing if they were alive or dead.

Malinka continued giving Jalby an ear-bashing. 'I've also asked the authorities what you're supposed to be doing instead of going to school. I don't believe this nonsense about you all helping Meribrayne with her research.'

The scientist had promised that she would keep the programmed children busy, but so far there hadn't been any evidence they would be doing a thing.

'You'll be back there studying with the rest of them, I can promise you!'

Jalby didn't dare argue. He even thought his aunt might have a point, but he wasn't going to tell her he suspected the machine had actually wiped everything he had ever learned from his brain.

Just then, his uncle ambled into the kitchen, as cheerful as ever. He slid his bulky frame onto a chair and the kitchen table creaked under the weight of his arms.

'So, ready for the big day, Jalby?'

Jalby nodded and tried not to look too glum.

'I've heard they're pitching you against your old classmates, just to see how bad the old education system really is. You are the future, Jalby. When you've shown them the results of brain programming, school will be obsolete.'

'It's not just me, Uncle Balton. They programmed four other children as well,' said Jalby, trying to take some of the attention off himself.

'You really do believe this rubbish, don't you Balton,' Aunt Malinka shouted.

'Well Malinka, if it weren't for science, astronauts would never have landed on Mars the other year, and we'd still be stuck in road cars, in traffic jams,' Balton replied.

This seemed to throw her for a moment. Clearly arriving on Mars was no more significant to her than finding a new out-of-town kitchen appliance centre, and she had never mastered hover transport.

'Well, we will see when he gets his results, won't we? But don't say I didn't warn you,' Malinka said frostily.

Uncle Balton eased himself up from his chair and stretched. He yawned loudly and wandered from the kitchen muttering to himself. Aunt Malinka fished several food tablets from the cupboard and placed them in the reconstitutor. Two seconds later there was a ping and she removed a plate of scrambled eggs on toast for Jalby's breakfast. Jalby had lost count of how often he had said he hated scrambled eggs. He even preferred reconstituted porridge. He turned his nose up at it.

'It'll do you good,' his aunt said. 'You know they only gave you those economy food pellets in hospital. These are finest quality – and you need building up.'

Faced with the prospect of total humiliation at school, he didn't care if he needed building up or not. He pushed the plate as far away as he could without his aunt seeing. Just then the intercom rang. The iris scanner beeped and a boy's face appeared on a large screen. It was Stuke, one of Jalby's schoolmates who had also been programmed.

After letting himself in, Stuke came bounding into the dining room, almost knocking over Malinka. He was a small, fair-haired boy, who seemed to be fed on something containing nuclear energy and looked like he spent precisely five seconds getting dressed.

In fact it only really took anyone 30 seconds to get dressed, as everyone wore a single layer of self-cleaning clothing. This layer would automatically adjust how warm it was, depending on the weather. Everyone was happy that they never needed to wash their clothes anymore. However, even though clothes didn't need washing, Stuke always managed to look scruffy somehow.

'How's it going, Jalby?' he yelled, as soon as he came in. 'Meribrayne told us what happened. We all thought you were a goner.'

Aunt Malinka left the room, shaking her head.

'I tried to visit you Jalby, but they said you needed rest,' Stuke went on. 'It sounded serious. You ready for the big test now? We're going to thrash them – they won't stand a chance against us. In a few days we'll be saying goodbye to school forever!'

Jalby shrugged his shoulders.

'How do you know the programming has worked, Stuke? Do you feel any cleverer?'

Stuke wasn't known for being the brightest student at school. If the programming had worked on him, they were bound to notice.

'Well, I can name all the rivers in Africa, and all the British prime ministers,' he replied.

'We did that two weeks ago in geography and history – of course you know them!' Jalby laughed.

Come to think of it, Jalby was starting to remember other things they had done this term. If the programming hadn't worked, at least it didn't seem to have wiped facts he had learned earlier.

'Well, I'm still up for showing them who's smartest now,' said Stuke.

'I don't think we've got much choice,' replied Jalby. 'Come on. Let's get going, before my aunt realises I've not eaten this stuff.'

Stuke cast a disapproving eye on Jalby's breakfast.

'You should get Phast-brex – you can eat them like sweets, no reconstitutor required, and they even clean your teeth while you're chewing them.'

'I'll look out for them. Might have to hide them from my aunt though.'

Jalby grabbed his bag, pushed a button on the front door and he and Stuke escaped from the flat.

'You have forgotten your coat,' an electronic voice informed Jalby. The door had an annoying scanner which analysed what he was wearing, and told him off if it didn't think he was properly dressed. Even though the scanner was several decades out of date, Malinka insisted on keeping it. It was from the time when people still wore several layers of clothing, and it didn't seem to realise it was more than thirty degrees outside. Jalby ignored it, as he always did, and they headed for the lift.

A long line of hover scooters were parked just outside the block of flats. Jalby took out his phone and remotely directed his scooter over to where they were standing. He pulled his helmet on and checked the guidance system in his visor.

'How's the bike going?' asked Stuke, jumping onto his own Hoverbyke 2060.

'It's still the fastest on or off the road,' Jalby smiled.

'Apart from mine!' Stuke laughed.

'We'll see about that!'

Stuke had modified their scooters so they could get around a bit more quickly. Normally children's scooters were designed to hover just half a metre above the ground, and could only follow set routes – usually routes which went to school or the library. If you tried to veer away from these routes, a control system pulled you back on course and sent a message to your parents or guardians, saying how bad you had been in trying to disobey the rules. You were usually banned from riding for a week, and had to take the hover bus to school instead. The scooters were limited to only 15 kilometres per hour, which was seen as fast enough for any child.

For adults, it was a different matter. Their scooters could go where they wanted, as fast as they liked. For some reason, they were trusted not to crash, even though there were regular reports of adults coming to a very sticky end. They could even fly, as long as they didn't go too high, which meant they could overtake children by flying over them.

Stuke was never happy about this. But one of the good things about Stuke was his ability to take things apart, modify them, and even put them back together again. It didn't take him long to work out how to disable the device that controlled his scooter. Before long he had also modified Jalby's scooter, and they regularly terrorised adults by flying centimetres above them. They could fly so fast that most adults never even noticed that it was a child who had almost taken their head off. Best of all was that they could avoid roads altogether – they were free to fly wherever they wanted, as long as they avoided the police patrols.

Word soon spread and Stuke now had a thriving business modifying other children's scooters, for a small fee of course. It was a business which had made him extremely popular. He also had a lot more pocket money than Jalby ever had.

The boys started up their scooters and flew off towards school, going slowly until they were out of sight. Jalby soon forgot all about the tests and programming as he weaved in and out of other traffic. Their daily commute was the best part of the day. Stuke's modifications also meant they could stay in bed for another fifteen minutes.

As they got near school, Stuke started jabbing his finger towards a girl on a scooter. It was Talia, the first person to be programmed.

She was heading to school for the same tests.

'Let's wake Talia up a bit,' shouted Stuke.

Jalby held back, in case any teachers were watching. Such things never occurred to Stuke though. A second later, he was racing less than a metre over Talia's head and then breaking hard, just before the school gate.

Unfortunately, he hadn't reckoned on Mr Prodorg, the maths teacher, arriving at exactly the same moment on his scooter. There was a sense of inevitability about it – a sickening crunch as the two scooters collided and Prodorg was thrown heavily to the ground. After the second bounce, he scrambled to his feet, visibly shaken. His rolls of flab still seemed to be rippling from the impact.

'What on Earth do you think you're playing at!' he shouted at Stuke as he dusted himself down. Somehow Stuke had stayed on his scooter, but he wasn't looking very pleased with himself now.

'I, I, I'm really sorry sir!' he stammered. 'I don't know what happened – it just seemed to have a mind of its own, and I lost control.'

'You don't need to tell me you lost control,' yelled the teacher, eyes blazing.

Just then a tall humanoid robot came scurrying over from the school. All humanoid robots were programmed to help humans and carry out first aid. Prodorg shooed the robot away and it turned and disappeared back inside the ugly building.

Talia caught up and looked about to explode at Stuke for dangerous low flying. She was thrusting out her chin as if it were a particularly lethal weapon. The look of fear in Stuke's face made her stop – he was already in big trouble.

'If this wasn't such a big day for you, I'd have you expelled,' Prodorg roared. 'However, as you're supposed to demonstrate you're ready to leave school anyway, I don't see there's much point.'

'No sir. Thank you sir,' Stuke mumbled.

'And make sure you get that scooter looked at!'

'Yes sir, I will sir.'

Prodorg limped off, pushing his scooter. His back light clattered to the ground but he didn't even notice. Stuke and the others didn't dare call him back.

'You could have killed me!' snarled Talia, when Mr Prodorg was out of earshot.

Talia was slender but towered over Stuke, and was nearly as tall as Jalby. She could get quite scary and people tried to stay out of her way when she was in a mood. Stuke's pride had taken a knock and, for once, he didn't know what to say.

'I'm sure he's learned his lesson,' Jalby said. 'Let's go and do these tests.'

Talia ignored Stuke and started quizzing Jalby about his accident at the laboratory.

'So what was it like? Was there any damage?' she asked eagerly.

'Well, the machine was destroyed, but my head seems ok. Not sure how well the programming worked though.'

A flicker of pleasure flashed across Talia's face, before she feigned a look of concern. It was no secret that she was highly ambitious. Everyone suspected she had pestered her parents so they would push for her to be programmed. As soon as she had been programmed, she had claimed she knew everything she needed to know about any subject. Talia was already clever, even before the programming, and Jalby was starting to get worried again.

'So you think we'll have no problems against the other students, do you?' he asked uncertainly.

'They, and the teachers, will be amazed,' Talia declared. 'Of course, it may not have worked perfectly for everyone,' she said slyly. Jalby and Stuke exchanged nervous glances. 'They said they couldn't exactly predict all the effects for each of us.'

'Did they?' said Jalby and Stuke together. This was news to them. They had probably fallen asleep during the lecture given by Meribrayne, when they were first told about the programming. Jalby's stomach suddenly felt like a turn of the century washing machine on spin cycle.

Chapter 4

Outside the school hall the mood was unusually lively considering everyone was waiting to be tested. Normally, before a test, most children shuffled around, feeling miserable.

None of the teachers had arrived yet – they were still drinking coffee in the staffroom, in an effort to face another long day at the school. Coffee had become so strong over the years you really could stand your spoon up in it, but it didn't stop most of the teachers having six cups of it every morning.

Several students were crowding round Dana and Bort, the other two children who had been programmed. Dana was a quiet girl, who kept herself to herself. She was not used to being the centre of attention and was trying to ignore everyone. Bort, on the other hand, was clenching his fists and getting red in the face. It was a comical sight. He was squaring up to Gorzon, a huge boy with arms bigger than most children's legs. Gorzon always looked like he wanted to squeeze someone's brains out with his bare hands. Sensible people stayed away from him.

'So, you reckon you'll beat us at Chinese do you?' laughed Gorzon.

'We'll beat you at everything!' shouted back Bort, as he squared up to the giant. However much he thrust out his chest, Bort looked ridiculous against Gorzon's formidable bulk.

Gorzon was normally top of the year for Chinese, but then he had lived in China for two years, after his father had set up a company there.

'I bet you'll all be back in infant school next week,' someone else yelled. Everyone laughed, except Dana and Bort.

Again Bort rose to the bait. 'You're just jealous you weren't chosen to be programmed.'

'Jealous? We like it here. We don't want to leave school,' piped up Wartbol, a geeky-looking boy, who probably really did enjoy school.

'Speak for yourself,' said Anton. 'I hardly like school, but it's where my mates are, and I'd miss hacking into the teachers' computers.'

Anton had a reputation for being a genius at computers, and anything technical, and he routinely tested the teachers' IT skills by putting viruses on their machines. His last virus froze the entire school computer system when Mr Blorton, the technology teacher, opened a message with the subject 'Beat your students at computing.'

Anton described his virus as a 'gift' to the teachers, saying it forced them to learn more about IT by figuring out how to repair the crippled network.

As Jalby and the others got closer, attention turned to them.

'Jalby, you're alive!' blurted out Gorzon in mock surprise. 'We thought the machine had blown your brains out!'

'Sorry to disappoint you,' muttered Jalby.

'Aren't you going to tell us what happened? We've been dying to find out,' Gorzon said sarcastically.

'Yeah, you could tell us in Chinese,' sniggered Dorf, one of Gorzon's closest allies.

Jalby felt stunned for a moment. Everyone suddenly seemed to go very quiet. Did they know that the machine had gone wrong during the Chinese programming?

'I think I'll save the Chinese for the test,' Jalby replied coldly.

'Ooh, feeling a bit sensitive are we?' Gorzon taunted.

'Leave it out, he's only just out of hospital,' said Talia.

'Ah, can't Jalby stand up for himself anymore?' Dorf mocked.

'Perhaps the programming has made him a bit, how do we say, soft in the head!' sneered Gorzon.

Jalby turned away so Gorzon and the others couldn't see the worried look on his face.

Finally Mr Gutborg arrived and started ushering everyone into the hall, where they spent ten minutes trying to find their desks. Gutborg taught Geography and sports. He might almost have been athletic, a few decades in the past, but now his slight frame and hunched shoulders made his body look like it would collapse in on itself at the slightest exertion. Unknown to the teacher, Anton had sent a virus which kept swapping everyone's electronic name-tags around every two seconds.

'Come on, hurry up!' yelled the teacher. 'How long can it take?'

Normally he was quite a patient teacher, but he had an even stronger whiff of coffee than usual this morning and was pacing around about as fast as his spindly legs would carry him.

'Sir, mine won't let me do anything,' moaned Lara.

'Try putting your password in again,' snapped Mr Gutborg.

'Oh, do I need my password?'

'Of course you do!'

Everyone laughed. Lara was always hopeless at computers.

Gorzon was sitting right behind Jalby, endlessly chanting 'Jalby's going to infant school!' until Stuke casually walked past

Gorzon's computer and pretended to trip over the power lead, causing it to drop to the floor. Gorzon's computer screen went black and he got up and headed for Stuke, teeth bared, looking as if he really wanted to cause some damage.

'Sit down and get ready!' Mr Gutborg barked, as Stuke walked back to his desk, whistling.

Eventually everyone stopped looking around aimlessly and sat with their electronic pens ready.

'First off, we've got a nice little maths test for you.' Mr Gutborg was smiling, but there was a malicious gleam in his eyes.

'Oh, not maths!' groaned Lara.

'That's right, everyone's favourite. Get ready to start. You've got forty minutes. Off you go.'

The first questions came on screen and Jalby immediately heard Gorzon scribbling away behind him. Jalby forced himself to look at the questions and realised they were quite easy – at least, the first page was. After a few minutes, he had scrawled all his answers onto the first screen and was calling up the second. He hadn't forgotten what he had been taught at all – it still seemed to be there! He sneaked a quick look to his left and saw Stuke looking quizzically at his screen. But, a moment later, even he was writing away, when normally he would be staring out the window, dreaming of scooters.

Jalby settled into a steady rhythm and even found himself enjoying it – but he would never admit this to anyone else. He realised though that, up to now, they had already learned how to answer all these questions in class. The real test was to come. There would be some questions only the brain-programmed students could answer. Perhaps then his answers would all be wrong.

On the fifth screen he started to see some unusual looking questions. He panicked. He didn't think he could answer them. Numbers and letters began to float before his eyes as he struggled to control his mind. He was sure they had never studied these at school, but he was still supposed to be able to answer them.

Just as he cast his eyes downwards, scanning for something he could answer, there was a feeling of blood rushing to his brain. All of a sudden he thought he could see how to answer the first of the difficult questions. His mind took on a life of its own, and his electronic pen was following, scribbling quickly on the screen. He was answering the questions. The programming seemed to be working!

Jalby heard a grunt from behind. Gorzon was starting to find the test tricky. There was a deep sigh and then Gorzon slid his chair backwards with a loud screech. Jalby could almost feel Gorzon's eyes boring into him. This was why Jalby was here. He would show Gorzon just how smart he was.

The maths test came and went, followed by English, history and all the other subjects they had ever studied. Jalby had never sat such a big test in all his life, and there were signs that the students were getting restless. Everyone, that is, except those who were programmed.

Jalby glimpsed Mr Gutborg stroll past Stuke shaking his head in disbelief. Here was Stuke scribbling away, looking completely calm, when normally he would be flicking elastic bands at Talia, his concentration dashed to pieces.

It was as Jalby was finishing what would have been a tricky geography question that his computer started behaving strangely. He was trying to write on the screen, but the words that appeared weren't what he had written with his electronic pen. He had never seen anything like it. Jalby tried to write the word 'century' several times, but, each time, something else appeared on screen. He stared in amazement as the words 'You will never defeat me!' came from his own pen. What was going on? Jalby waited a moment and tried writing again.

'The brain programming has not worked – all your answers are wrong,' appeared this time, when Jalby thought he had written something about out-of-town shopping centres in the twentieth century. Jalby tried writing 'Who are you?' but there was no reply.

He was worried now. Perhaps all his answers were wrong, when he had only thought the tests were going well. And now his own computer seemed to be rebelling against him. Again he waited a few moments.

This time, the computer was getting personal.

'Do you miss your parents, Jalby?' it wrote. 'Do you wonder where they are? What's it like not knowing? They can't help you now. You can't go crying to mummy. You are a failure, Jalby. You can't concentrate on anything. You will be at school forever. Your answer to that last question was rubbish. Stop wasting everyone's time…'

Jalby was having trouble concentrating now. He was starting to sweat. He was close to panic. He started to remember when things were better – when his parents were still around, and when he was still good at things. He was useless now. Even the computer was telling him so.

Jalby tore his eyes away from the screen and gazed through the window.

'Is there a problem Jalby?' Mr Gutborg asked.

'N, No, sir,' Jalby stammered.

'Good. Well, let's have you carrying on.'

Jalby managed to calm himself down. When he tried writing again, his computer seemed back to normal. He deleted the sentences that it, or something, had just written. He finished the geography question. This time, his words were his own, but feelings of doubt still nagged at the back of his mind.

The last test was Chinese. Jalby knew that Gorzon would be looking forward to this one. It was Gorzon's chance to show everyone at school, especially Jalby, just how good he was at the most difficult subject. If Jalby felt uneasy before, he was dreading the Chinese test.

They got quickly underway. Again Jalby heard Gorzon scribbling away on his screen, as if his life depended on it. Jalby could picture the smile on Gorzon's face.

In all the subjects so far, Jalby seemed to have done the first screens without needing the programming at all – it was stuff that they all should have known. This time it was different. There were questions that should have been easy – 'Translate "How are you?" into Chinese.' Jalby stared dumbfounded at the screen, unable to answer them. The next question was 'Translate "I live in London"' – but what was the word for 'live'? Jalby didn't have a clue. Perhaps he really would be coming back to school, to rejoin the Chinese lessons from the beginning.

He scanned through another page, desperately trying to find something he could answer. Suddenly he stopped. Something amazing happened. There, before his eyes, was a difficult passage in Chinese he had to translate into English. Somehow, he could do it! 'Now, in the second half of the twenty-first century, Chinese is just as widely taught as English...,' started the passage. Jalby tried to understand what was going on. When the machine blew up, it must have wiped only the simple things from his mind. He knew the difficult stuff, but he didn't even know how to say his name!

Before long, there were the familiar sounds of Gorzon getting worked up again. 'How can I answer this?' Jalby heard him mutter through clenched teeth. 'Shh!' hissed Mr Gutborg. Jalby couldn't help smiling.

When Mr Gutborg finally announced 'Time's up,' there was a huge sigh of relief. Chairs and tables screeched as students jumped up. 'Time's up I said!' bellowed the teacher, whilst bearing down on Lara. 'Oh, sorry sir!' she said innocently.

Noise levels became deafening as everyone started swapping answers. 'No, that's not right you idiot,' Jalby heard someone saying. 'Water freezes at zero!' Clearly someone didn't even know the basics.

Stuke came bouncing over to Jalby. 'How'd it go? Reckon you'll be back at school?' He was more enthusiastic than Jalby had ever seen him after a test. Normally he was straight out the door as quickly as humanly possible.

'Not too sure,' said Jalby. 'I had one or two strange things happen on my computer.'

'Like what?' asked Stuke, raising his eyebrows.

Jalby explained about the mysterious writing on his screen.

'Wow, so you think your answers could be a load of rubbish?'

'Could be,' replied Jalby. 'Guess we'll find out soon.'

All the tests were to be marked by the school's central computer, which could read even the worst electronic handwriting.

Just then Anton strode over looking very pleased with himself. 'You owe me one, Jalby!'

'How come?'

'You couldn't see Gorzon fiddling with your computer after he got bored.'

'What!' replied Jalby and Stuke in unison.

'Gorzon's got hold of one of these ghostskriptas. They're forbidden!'

Jalby looked confused, as he often did when Anton started

talking about technical things. Anton took out a tiny device with an antenna – so small that a teacher wouldn't even notice it.

'You link it to your computer, point the antenna at someone else's computer, write your message, and the message appears on their screen when they start writing – very spooky.'

Jalby felt relieved for a moment, and then angry, as he thought of Gorzon laughing at him behind his back.

'So, how did you stop him?' asked Stuke.

'Easy. I told him I'd hacked into his computer with my ghostskripta and knew exactly what he was up to. He didn't even guess it was me!'

'That must have put him off,' Jalby smiled.

'I told him I'd wipe all his answers with a virus, and make him look like the school dunce.'

'Wow, can a ghostskripta do that?' Stuke asked.

'No, but Gorzon doesn't know that. You know he loses interest in any of his gadgets after five minutes. The guy's clueless!' Stuke and Jalby laughed.

They were just leaving the school when Bort hurried past them, as white as a sheet.

'You alright Bort?' Stuke shouted after him.

Bort ignored them all, ran down the steps and roared off on his scooter.

'What's with him? Looks like he's seen an alien!' said Anton.

'Dunno, but it doesn't look good,' replied Stuke.

'I'm going after him. You coming Stuke?' asked Jalby.

'Yeah, let's go see what's up.'

They ran over to their scooters and almost collided with Talia and Dana.

'What's the hurry, Jalby? Can't wait to leave school?' Talia asked. She was looking very happy with herself after the day's tests.

'Sorry Talia, got to go!' yelled Jalby, as he and Stuke jumped on to their scooters.

The girls stared after them as they disappeared into the distance.

Chapter 5

They found Bort at his favourite place – the robot ball park. A group of boys were playing basketball with a team of robots. The residential robots at the park were especially good at basketball and seemed to be thrashing the boys. Normally, Bort would join in – he was one of the best players at school and could sometimes even get past the robots. Instead, he was sitting under a palm tree, staring into space.

'What's up Bort?' Jalby asked as they approached.

Bort looked up slowly. 'The brain programming. I don't think it's worked,' he moaned.

'How do you know?' asked Stuke.

'Yeah, surely we'll only know tomorrow. When we get the results,' said Jalby encouragingly.

'I could only answer the easy stuff. You know, the first few screens on each test. The rest of it I didn't have a clue. Couldn't even try to answer them.'

Jalby and Stuke glanced at each other awkwardly. It was difficult to know what to say.

'Do you think you remembered the stuff you were taught normally?' asked Jalby thoughtfully.

'Yeah, I think so.'

'So, at least it doesn't look like the programming mucked about with your brain,' Jalby continued.

'Yeah, and you said you didn't want to leave school anyway!' said Stuke.

'Yes, but I was just getting used to the idea of not going back!' complained Bort.

'Come on. Let's play the robots at basketball. It'll take your mind off it,' suggested Jalby.

When they joined the other boys, three more robots filed on to the court to make up the numbers – it never seemed to matter if there were more than five players on each side. The score was already robots 9, boys 3, and Jalby suspected the robots had been programmed to let in one basket, so the boys wouldn't give up too easily. The two teams let Jalby and his friends warm up, and then they continued the same game.

One good thing about playing robots was that they always played fair – you may not stand a chance of beating them, but they didn't understand the concept of cheating. Jalby didn't think they understood anything really – they just bounced the ball round moving obstacles and scored baskets. It was all quite mechanical. Each time a robot scored, they all emitted a tinny fanfare and the scoring robot did a back-flip. It was then back to business, to score the next basket – usually only a few seconds later.

Bort seemed to be leaving his troubles behind as soon as he got on the court. He lived for basketball, and it was always good fun trying to beat the robots.

A robot was soon bouncing the ball quickly past Jalby. Jalby tried a block, but the robot spun round and threw the ball in a fast low pass to another perfectly placed robot. A few more bounces, an enormous leap, and then 'ktang', another basket, and another back-flip. Jalby was never very good at basketball, but he seemed to be playing even worse than usual. Stuke passed the ball, Jalby failed to catch it and then collided with Bort. They both ended up in a heap on the court. Bort was enjoying the game but even he couldn't seem to work his usual magic. He sprang for the ball, missed, fell and took a robot down with him. Bort scrambled up looking embarrassed. One of the other boys stood shaking his head. The worst moment was when Stuke missed an easy shot at the basket, stumbled backwards, knocked over Jalby and trod on his leg.

'Argh!' Jalby yelled. 'Have you forgotten how to play?'

The robots scored three more baskets, but then something

unusual started to happen. Jalby was bouncing the ball. Normally he would lose it after only a few bounces, but this time he was bouncing it faster than ever. He even managed to spin round, outwitting two robots. He gave a high pass to Stuke. Stuke found himself outpacing a robot. He bounced the ball quickly, only inches from the ground. Bort was right there. He took possession and ran circles round another robot, which just stood there as if it was confused. Another robot tried a block, but Bort was too quick. He spun round, leaped and 'ktang!' The boys all cheered. Bort was smiling again.

The robots fought back and scored the next few baskets, but then the boys were back on top. Bort scored again and again. Even Jalby and Stuke got baskets, after blisteringly fast runs across the court. The robots started to stand there, as if unsure which way to move. They clumsily tried to reach out for the ball, grabbing at thin air. The other boys looked at Bort, Jalby and Stuke in amazement. What was going on? The three boys were the same age as they were, but they were playing better than the robots.

Suddenly one of the robots stood in the middle of the court, motionless. It seemed to have had enough. Stuke elegantly bounced the ball past it, there was a deafening bang, a flash, an acrid smell filled the air and the robot crumpled to its knees. Black smoke started billowing from its head. The boys cheered again as the robots looked on. This was not supposed to happen. Final score: robots 29, boys 37.

'Would someone mind explaining what happened there?' asked Stuke, as they walked back towards their scooters.

'Beats me!' said Bort. 'We were hopeless at the beginning. I've never played a game like that before.'

'Me neither!' said Jalby.

'You could hardly even bounce the ball before,' Stuke reminded Jalby.

'Hey, I wasn't that bad!' retorted Jalby. 'Ok, I'd never have made the team…'

'You will now!' exclaimed Bort.

'Do you reckon they'll allow us back to play if we leave school?' Stuke asked.

'Dunno,' replied Jalby. 'But I reckon I'm going professional!'

'Yeah, right!' said Stuke.

'What will you do anyway, with all this free time?' asked Bort.

'I'm not sure. We're supposed to be helping at the lab, but I don't think the scientists have really thought about that,' replied Jalby.

'We can ride around all day, and tune even more scooters,' suggested Stuke.

'Yeah, great!' said Jalby sarcastically. He could see how riding and tuning scooters all day could get a little boring.

Suddenly, Gorzon and Dorf appeared from nowhere, with Smoyd, another mean looking character from school. The three biggest boys in the school usually hung around together, looking for trouble.

'So, you reckon you're great at basketball now do you?' snarled Dorf.

'Well, we showed the robots how to play, didn't we,' replied Stuke, looking round at Bort and Jalby.

'We sure did. Why don't you try playing them? Tell us the score later,' said Bort.

'We'll play them when we feel like playing them,' grunted Smoyd.

'First, there's the small problem with the robot over there,' continued Gorzon. They all looked round to where the robot lay at the side of the court, smoke still coming out of its head.

'I think we need to report this vandalism to the authorities. And perhaps also this business of yours with the scooters,' said Gorzon threateningly.

'You wouldn't dare report us,' said Stuke. 'No-one would ever speak to you again!'

'People speak to us when we tell them to speak to us!'

'Listen to Gorzon, he thinks he's some kind of mafia boss!' joked Stuke.

This was not a wise thing to say. Just then, there was a loud crack as Smoyd's huge fist connected with Stuke's jaw. A second later, Stuke was lying on the ground while Jalby was grappling with Gorzon and Dorf. He managed to break free from Gorzon's grip, just in time to avoid Dorf's fist pummelling into his face. Instead, the fist embedded itself into Gorzon's nose with a sickening squelch.

'Ahh! You stupid fool!' yelled Gorzon.

Jalby turned to see Bort laying into Smoyd. Smoyd was sluggishly trying to defend himself, but Bort was at least twice as quick. He even seemed to know where Smoyd was going to strike next. Smoyd swung at Bort's head – a huge swing that would have taken his head off – but Bort easily ducked out the way, and followed up with a lightning punch at Smoyd's jaw. Smoyd stumbled back, dazed.

'Look out!' Bort shouted at Jalby.

Dorf lashed out viciously, but Jalby deflected his fist and neatly stepped out of the way. He followed with a jab at Dorf's stomach. Dorf started groaning loudly. He was doubled up in pain.

'Geddim!' screamed Gorzon, clutching his nose.

Smoyd had the look of a maniac as he charged. Jalby wasn't sure who he was heading for, but he had a particularly nasty glint in his eye. As Jalby and Bort were deciding which way to run, Smoyd's eyes widened in horror. Stuke had woken up and expertly swept Smoyd's feet from under him in a magnificent flying tackle. Smoyd reached out to save himself, but it was no good. His massive bulk knocked the wind clean out of him as he landed.

'Come on, time to go!' yelled Jalby.

They ran to their scooters, jumped on even more quickly than usual, and took off. Gorzon and Dorf were staggering around, looking on in amazement. Smoyd was still scrabbling around in the dirt, spitting out mud.

'Wow! How did we get out of that one?' shouted Stuke above the din of the motors.

'No idea! No-one else has survived a fight with them!' shouted back Jalby.

'It's alright for you. You're both leaving school. You don't have to see them anymore!' complained Bort.

'Don't worry, they won't bother any of us again,' replied Jalby.

'Glad you're so sure,' said Bort.

'Ah, come on. All you have to do is give us a call. We'll come and sort them out,' Stuke said defiantly. 'Besides you don't even know your test results yet – you don't know you've failed.'

Bort was already resigned to going back to school, but he was looking forward to some interesting basketball matches.

Chapter 6

The following day was results day. It was nine o'clock and there was pandemonium in the hall. Students were pushing and shoving, eager to see their scores on the large screen. Several teachers were trying to keep order, but it was no use.

'That can't be right!' yelled Wartbol.

Others shoved him out of the way so they could see.

'No way have I got scores like these. I want to speak to the head!' squealed Lara, after seeing how bad her results were.

'Quiet!' yelled Mrs Zenton, the history teacher. 'The computer which marks the tests does not make mistakes, unlike students!' she croaked, hoarse from shouting.

'But Jalby and the others have never studied most of the stuff on the tests!' Lara complained.

For once, she had made a good point, and Mrs Zenton seemed to struggle for words.

'Well go and speak to the head then!' she blurted out.

Jalby and Stuke fought their way to the front, desperate to see how they had done.

'Jalby, how did you manage it?' someone demanded.

He finally saw the numbers spread across the screen. Maths 100%, History 96%, Science 97%. He was amazed. One subject after another, it was the same story. Then he remembered – Chinese! He scanned along quickly, his breath quickening. Would he still need lessons? There it was. Chinese 90%. He had dropped a few marks, but it wasn't bad, not bad at all!

Several of his friends patted him on the back. 'Way to go Jalby!' said one excitedly.

Jalby looked round for Stuke. He was right behind, smiling and holding up his arms as if his team had just won the Blorgon World Basketball Championships.

'Stuke! Stuke!' People were chanting. His results were not far behind Jalby's – except for Chinese, where he had actually got 95%. Jalby caught sight of Gorzon scowling at them. He quickly found Gorzon's Chinese result – only 65%! Gorzon turned and pushed his way out of the crowd, before disappearing down the corridor.

Talia and Dana appeared from the crowd. Talia was beaming. 'Well done!' she said. 'Looks like we pulled it off! Sorry about your Chinese result though, Jalby!'

'Hey, 90%'s a good mark! Look at what Gorzon got, and he lived there!' said Jalby. Everyone laughed. Overall, Talia had scored about the same as Jalby, apart from getting 98% in Chinese.

Just then, Bort came across, looking glum.

'Well done guys. Afraid I didn't do too well,' he said.

Jalby glanced across at the screen and just caught sight of a few of Bort's marks. He hadn't done any worse than the other students in the school, but the programming clearly hadn't worked.

'Sorry about that Bort,' said Jalby gently. 'I guess the technology still needs working on.'

'You could say that,' replied Bort, trying to smile.

'We'll get Professor Meribrayne to rebuild the machine, and then you can have another go!' said Talia encouragingly.

'Not sure that's likely to happen after what happened to you, Jalby,' Bort said.

'Yeah, I reckon school's safer!' said Stuke.

Until now, Dana had not said a word.

'Well, I guess I'll be off then,' she said, before disappearing through the crowds of over-excited students.

'She's as fun as ever!' said Stuke sarcastically.

'She's probably tired. Maybe she didn't sleep last night, thinking about the tests,' Talia replied.

'I bet she's gone off to study,' said Stuke.

'Study what!?' asked Jalby and Talia together.

'Ah, good point!' laughed Stuke, feeling a little daft.

Jalby wondered if the programming had really changed anything. They still seemed to be the same people, and Stuke didn't appear to be any brighter. Perhaps they had just been programmed how to pass tests, and they would still be clueless out in the adult world.

'Of course, if you'd like to carry on studying, don't let us stop you!' Talia said jokingly.

Suddenly Jalby remembered he had to go back to the institute. He didn't really think it was necessary now but Meribrayne had seemed keen to see him again.

'Sorry to be boring, but I've got to visit the professor for a check-up.'

'But you know your brain wasn't damaged – look at your results!' Talia said.

'Perhaps they were just lucky guesses!' Jalby smiled.

'Yeah, and you might have a bit of that programmer stuck behind your eyes!' Stuke started to mime someone struggling to pull a large shard of metal from the side of Jalby's head.

'Great – thanks for reminding me Stuke! See you all later.'

It was a ten-minute ride to the institute – an ultramodern structure with dark tinted glass, designed, Jalby thought, so it was difficult to see what was going on inside. It always took Jalby a moment to remember which of the glass panels was the entrance. He pressed on a panel – nothing happened. He pressed on a second panel, looked at the glass, and his iris was scanned. A second later, a secret door slid open and he stepped inside before it closed quickly behind him.

Usually Jalby enjoyed going to the institute, but he was thinking about his experience with the brain programmer, in one of the laboratories upstairs.

Inside, a robot sat at a large desk – one of Meribrayne's recent attempts to replace the incompetent receptionist.

'Meribrayne is in her office,' the robot droned.

Hello to you too, thought Jalby.

The robot pressed a button and a section of the floor lifted up, carrying Jalby through the ceiling into the professor's large room.

Meribrayne was pacing about, looking agitated.

'Ah, Jalby, you've come. Please take a seat.'

Something didn't seem right to Jalby. He scanned the office. No change here, he thought. He had last been in the office a few weeks before the programming, with his uncle and aunt, whilst Meribrayne briefed them in more detail about the procedure. Scientific journals and papers were still strewn across her grand desk, and heavy, serious looking books stretched almost to the ceiling. Jalby wondered how she was ever able to find anything, without sending things cascading to the floor. Meribrayne was a woman with other priorities than tidiness. She also seemed curiously old-fashioned for someone who was a top scientist. Most people, except Meribrayne and Jalby's aunt, didn't even bother with books anymore.

Jalby sat down and waited for Meribrayne to gather her thoughts.

'I'm afraid something's come up,' the professor said in a worried voice.

Jalby's heart missed a beat.

'I can't give you a check-up today,' Meribrayne continued. 'Someone hacked into the system last night – they copied documents about brain programming.'

Jalby settled back into his chair. He, at least, seemed to be in the clear for the moment. 'I'm afraid I can't tell you very much, Jalby, but I think that someone will try to use brain programming for their own purposes.

'Perhaps it was just someone who wanted to program himself - or herself,' said Jalby thoughtfully.

'Unfortunately I don't think so. The programming can do more than just educate people. You may have already noticed other, more physical effects.'

Jalby thought of the basketball game and the fight with Gorzon.

'So, the programming can improve our physical abilities – our coordination?' asked Jalby excitedly.

'Yes, after a bit of practice. But it has the potential to do far more.'

Jalby's mind was racing, trying to imagine what it was capable of.

'I'm in a very difficult position,' continued the professor. 'I need to find out who's taken copies of those files.'

'Do you have any idea who it was?'

'I have an idea who may be behind it. But I don't have any proof.' Meribrayne rubbed her forehead and sighed.

'I want you and the others to keep out of sight as much as possible. Don't tell anyone else about the programming.'

'Of course, professor.'

Jalby was wondering what was going on at the institute. He said goodbye to the professor and descended back to the entrance hall, where the robot receptionist was trying to answer a telephone call.

'What is your name? Repeat, what is your name?' The robot seemed to be having trouble.

Jalby headed for the entrance and left quickly before the robot tried to say anything to him. He looked back at the low squat shape of the institute. The dark glass seemed to be inviting him to test himself. He stood there for a few seconds, trying to pluck up the courage, daring himself to do it. Suddenly he ran straight at the building, launched himself off the ground and did a back flip off the wall. He was amazed – he had never done anything other than a handstand before.

He wasn't sure what to do next, but he wanted to do something. His mind was a mix of excitement and fear as he headed back across town.

Chapter 7

Jalby was selective about what he told his aunt Malinka. It was always better not to tell her too much anyway. He'd only been home about two seconds before she asked him about his test results.

'So go on. What did you get? Were they a total disaster?'

'Well, they weren't bad,' Jalby said slyly.

He was almost tripped up by the vacuum cleaner which was automatically scurrying back and forth while his aunt was watching TV. For a moment it seemed to have forgotten it was supposed to avoid obstacles.

'What do you mean "not bad"?' Malinka screeched. 'If they're not bad, you can go back to school until you know the subjects properly. What did I tell you about brain programming!?'

'I got 100% in maths, 96% in history, 97% in science, and the rest were similar.'

It took his aunt a few seconds to register. It was as if she had been hit over the head with a particularly heavy plank of wood.

'What did you get in Chinese?'

She had to ask.

'90%' he replied warily.

'Oh, so you dropped a few points there then. Do you have to resit it?'

'Auntie, Gorzon only got 65%, and he lived in China!' he protested.

'That Gorzon's a good for nothing anyway,' his aunt said. 'Don't go comparing yourself to the likes of him.'

'No auntie.'

'Anyway, I decided to arrange your Chinese books properly, upstairs, so you can find them easily. Half an hour study and then go to bed.'

'Yes auntie. I'll go and read them now,' he lied.

His books had been gathering dust for years. He only ever used his computer for studying, but even this seemed outdated now.

He went upstairs, lay on his bed and started thinking about what the professor had said. What were these other effects she was talking about, and what could be so dangerous about them?

He thought back to the basketball game and the fight and chuckled to himself. In some way, the programming had improved their physical capabilities beyond recognition. Bort was better than ever at basketball, even if the programming hadn't given him an education. Jalby himself had never been able to bounce a basketball more than three times in a row before. He had never even thrown a punch in anger. If all the effects were like this, life could be even more fun, especially with people like Gorzon around.

Jalby reached for his laptop. His computer made the usual whirring sound as it decided whether to break down again.

'Find Professor Meribrayne,' he ordered.

'No items match your search criterion,' the machine replied.

'Find brain programming.' Again nothing!

That was odd. Meribrayne had proudly shown her website at the school, when she was explaining the new technique. This time he tried the institute. The website was still there, but there was nothing about brain-programming – it was as if all knowledge of it had been wiped away. Meribrayne really did seem to want no one else to know about her prize invention. He wondered how Anton managed to hack onto computer systems so easily. IT had also been programmed into his brain – perhaps it would help. He navigated to a page which asked for a password but got no further. Of course, he thought, if there was one computer system he wouldn't be able to access it would be the institute's – the scientists would have made sure of that.

Just then, his phone bleeped. It was a message from Meribrayne. At least, it was part of a message – Jalby, they've got me. Stay away from the lab. They will… The message ended.

Jalby tried calling her. Her phone was dead. She had told him she would always have her phone on, just in case any of them had any problems after the programming. He tried again five minutes later – nothing.

It was already dark outside. What would Stuke be up to? Probably not a lot. Probably revelling in the fact he would never have to go to school again. Jalby had to tell him and the others what had happened.

He picked up his phone, whispered 'Stuke', and the phone called his friend's number.

'Hey Jalby, how's it going?'

Jalby could see a 3-D image of Stuke on his screen – he was playing a computer game Jalby hadn't seen before.

'I got this great game to celebrate our freedom. Can you see it? In this one, you get to genetically modify an alien, so that it's indestructible.'

Jalby could see an extremely ugly alien – Stuke's creation –

laying waste to a secondary school as the school children looked on cheering.

'Yeah Stuke – it looks great. Listen, do you want to meet at the arcade in town? I've got something to tell you.'

Jalby thought the amusement arcade would be more likely to get Stuke out of his house.

'Yeah, I've heard their latest game is brilliant – a real simulation of the Mars landing.'

'Ok, see you there in half an hour.'

Jalby slipped downstairs to find his aunt glued to another reality TV show. Contestants actually thought they had been transported back in time to the year 2000. The programme tried to recreate a world with cars, ancient-looking computers that still had keyboards, and food that hadn't quite been processed beyond recognition. Aunt Malinka was sitting a metre from the TV, her mouth wide open – she didn't seem to realise it was all a hoax. 'Auntie, I'm off to bed early, I'm tired.'

'Ok dear. Sleep well,' she said, without removing her eyes from the TV.

Back in his room, Jalby picked up his phone, switched on the scooter's video camera and steered it slowly up the side of the building to the back of the flat, leaving it hovering outside his window. Gently, he opened the window, brought the scooter closer and leaped on, while trying to forget that the ground was fifteen metres below. The scooter dropped slightly but then recovered, before Jalby opened the throttle and flew off to town.

Stuke was already at the arcade when Jalby arrived. The Mars simulator looked just like the actual landing in 2055, until a giant alien with twelve arms started pounding at the landing craft.

Stuke unleashed several rockets at the giant. 'Die! Die!' he was yelling.

'Very realistic!' said Jalby. 'Good to see you in training for the next Mars landing.'

'Oh, hi Jalby. Just one, more, alien – no, he's got me. I'm down!'

Stuke's landing craft nose-dived towards the red planet and burst into flames.

'So, Jalby – what's up? Not heard anything from Meribrayne yet about that research we're supposed to be helping with?'

'I'm going to tell you something important. Can you keep it secret?' Jalby asked seriously.

'You know me. I kept it secret when we sabotaged the head's computer.'

Anton had adapted their phones so that he, Stuke and Jalby could all lock on to the head teacher's computer and transmit different viruses to it, all at the same time. His virus software couldn't cope and his computer blew up.

'Yeah, but that was because we'd all have got into trouble – including you,' Jalby replied.

'Ok. Anyway, what is it?'

Jalby told him about his meeting with Meribrayne, but Stuke looked sceptical.

'I can't see how the programming could be abused,' he said. 'I reckon Meribrayne just wants to keep the device to herself, so she can make loads of money from it.'

'Bit strange how the website has gone though, don't you think?' asked Jalby. 'It's not as if it had any information on it that was technical. You know, anything that would help you to actually make a programmer.'

'I suppose you're right,' agreed Stuke, 'and you'd think she'd want everyone to know she'd invented it. But what can we do?'

'We have to do something. Her message sounds like she needs our help. I think she's in danger,' Jalby replied. He thought for a moment. 'I'd like to take another look at the laboratory – when no one's there.'

'She told us to stay away. And how are we going to get in? It's impossible to get past the robot at reception – we can't just walk in uninvited!'

Stuke was starting to sound as if the programming had knocked some sense into him.

'I can get in. The entrance should still recognise our iris scans. What we need is a diversion,' said Jalby. 'Robots are programmed to help humans, if we have an accident.'

'I'm not sure I like the sound of this,' muttered Stuke.

'Do you think you could crash your scooter outside the institute?' asked Jalby.

'Oh no! Not another crash!'

'Oh come on. It just has to look good – like a proper accident. It doesn't have to be a proper accident. You don't even need to damage your scooter! The robot will have to come out to help you. You were programmed the day before Meribrayne got the robot at reception, right?'

'Yes, that's right.'

'So the robot won't recognise you or get suspicious,' Jalby continued. 'A few seconds later I can then slip in through the front door.'

'And if I bust my scooter, will you get me a new one?'

'Is that all you care about? Your scooter?' asked Jalby.

Stuke thought for a while. 'Let's try Meribrayne again.'

Jalby was doubtful, but he got his phone out and called.

'It's still dead. Hold on – there's a message. Her number's not recognised. We can't contact her!'

'Ok. Let's do it,' said Stuke. 'Wait a minute though. What about the security cameras, and the infra-red sensors. And all the people working there?'

'I've thought about that,' said Jalby calmly. 'We get Anton to hack into the institute's computers and do his stuff, like he's done before.'

Anton would hopefully be able to lock on to the computer system remotely through Jalby's phone, and then find and disable the security system. What would happen when the robot found the cameras disabled was impossible to tell – it was a risk.

'Anton likes a challenge,' Jalby continued. 'Remember that time when he broke into school?' he asked Stuke.

'Yeah, and he went at night, when no-one else was around.'

'Exactly. So we're going to do the same tomorrow night. If we go at midnight, perhaps no one will be around.'

'Sounds like some sort of a plan. But don't I get to come into the institute too?' asked Stuke, disappointed.

'Afraid not. Can't see how I can get you in after your crash.'

'Well, I'll probably be off to hospital anyway,' moaned Stuke.

'You'll be fine. I'll give Anton a call now and tell him the plan.'

Jalby left Stuke playing the Mars simulator and thought about what to say to Anton, without saying too much. Best to give as little away as possible, he thought.

Anton's animated face appeared on Jalby's phone. From the reflections on his glasses, Jalby guessed he was at his computer, instant messaging someone, or hacking into a system.

'Hey Jalby, how's freedom!?'

'Anton, I've got a little job for you. Remember the laboratory where my brain was programmed?'

Jalby explained his idea and Anton's face lit up.

'I've never hacked into a research institute before. Should be fun!'

'Do you think you can do it?'

'I reckon so. It'll probably be a bit tougher than usual. But these scientists are more interested in their own research – not security. Leave it to me!'

'Great. I'll call you again tomorrow, before Stuke has his "accident".'

'I could leave them a virus as well – just something to say hello...' Anton suggested.

'No, just deal with the security – nothing else,' Jalby replied.

He headed home. It was already getting late. He didn't need to go back to school in the morning, but he guessed his aunt would still try to wake him up at half six, and he needed some sleep before the following night.

Chapter 8

They headed quickly through the city streets on their scooters. It was late the following night, getting on for midnight, and their adrenaline was building up the closer they got to the institute. Jalby was racking his brains, trying to think of anything he had forgotten. Stuke was silent for once, thinking how he could create a convincing diversion without wrecking his beloved scooter.

They turned into the familiar wide avenue and stopped, checking for any signs of life. The street was quite far out of town and the institute was the only building of any size on it. There was no-one around and the building was in darkness, except for the area near the entrance, where Jalby knew the robot would be on guard.

You couldn't normally get past a robot: they didn't need to eat or drink, and they wouldn't fall asleep. If they were programmed to stand guard, that's what they would do, endlessly. They even knew if their batteries were running low, and could plug themselves in for a recharge. The institute's robot was probably recharging right now, whilst still keeping watch on a dozen monitors at once, and with enough power in reserve to bound off down the corridor and arrest any intruders. Although Professor Meribrayne's robot lacked the finer points of telephone etiquette, it was one of the latest models and could easily out-run a human. It could also see in the dark.

Jalby was starting to have second thoughts. He wasn't sure how much time he would need to get in the building while the robot was distracted. He also wasn't really sure what he was looking for, and he still had no idea how he would get out again. All Stuke had to worry about was crashing his scooter convincingly, without killing himself.

Jalby got out his phone and whispered, 'Anton'. There was no answer. 'Come on Anton,' Jalby muttered.

He tried again and, this time, Anton's face appeared on screen.

'Anton, are you nearly ready?'

'Ready when you are. Have you located the system?'

'Not yet, I need to get closer. Stuke's looking a bit worried though. I'll call you back. You ok Stuke?' Jalby asked.

'Yeah. So you want me to crash right in front of the entrance?'

'That's right. And if you could make lots of noise.'

'What sort of noise?'

'You know. Like you've crashed sort of noise. A bit of screaming – I'm sure you can make it look good. Didn't you audition for drama at school?'

'Yes, but I didn't have to speak.'

'You don't have to speak. Just scream!'

Jalby edged round the corner near the entrance and knelt in the shadows. He took out his phone and punched in a code. A few seconds later, his phone beeped quietly. It had locked on to the institute's computer system. Jalby called Anton and this time he answered immediately.

'Ok, just give me a minute. Just finding their security. No, not there – that was their staff restaurant menu. They've got sausages tomorrow – real food – I want to work there!'

'Come on Anton!' said Jalby.

'Ok, here we are. They don't normally advertise their security systems. This must be it, though. Cameras, and infra-red sensors. Just got to work out how to disable them now.'

'Don't disable them yet Anton. Wait until I say.'

Suddenly there was the whine of an approaching scooter. Jalby watched as Stuke swung out into the road and picked up speed. A few seconds later he came careering past and, just in front of the entrance, he leaned over to one side and stamped on the brakes. The scooter spun round sharply, catapulting Stuke into a bush.

Jalby was stunned: Stuke had either made it look really good, or he really had crashed badly. There was a horrendous crunch as the scooter wrapped itself round a post at the side of the road. It sounded expensive. Then there were the screams. Stuke could scream really well. His loud shrieks pierced the still, night air.

Just as Jalby was wondering whether to go and help, he heard the door of the institute slide open. The plan seemed to be working. The robot bounded over to where Stuke lay tangled in the bush.

'Argh! Argh! Help!'

Jalby couldn't tell if Stuke was really injured, but at least he could speak – and the robot would be programmed to do first aid. Stuke was in good hands.

'Anton, are you there?' Jalby whispered hurriedly into his phone.

'Yeah. What's that racket? Is someone dying?'

'It's Stuke. He'll be alright. Can you disable the cameras and sensors? Now!'

There was the sound of tapping. It seemed to go on for a very long time.

'I'm having a few problems,' Anton said finally.

'What sort of problems?'

'The cameras aren't responding. I can't switch them off!'

Moving around the institute with the security cameras on would be hopeless – Jalby would be spotted instantly when the robot returned.

'I'm not on the system,' Anton said suddenly. 'Your phone's not locked on anymore!'

The robot was tending to Stuke only twenty metres away. It would be back any second – unless Stuke really did need first aid.

Jalby took a deep breath and crept to the entrance, hoping it would still recognise his iris scan. He pressed his thumb against the door and looked towards the glass. There was a buzzing sound and a second later he was inside. He leaned over the reception desk and saw dozens of monitors. Each monitor had an infra-red image of a darkened room or corridor in the vast building. He couldn't get much closer to the security system than this. This time his phone locked on to the system immediately.

'Anton, is this any good now?'

'That's good. Must be a better connection,' Anton replied.

A few seconds later, Jalby saw the security monitors go black one by one. The cameras were disabled.

'Good work Anton. Speak later.'

Jalby had to move quickly through the hall. He knew he would be vulnerable in the glare of the lights. He needed to find his way to Meribrayne's office. Using the lift would be out of the question – too obvious, and he didn't even know where the controls were. He bolted down a passageway and almost ran headlong down a flight of stairs. 'Up, not down,' thought Jalby.

He suddenly jumped back with fright – there was someone looking straight at him, towering over him. The man didn't move - he just seemed to stand there. Jalby breathed a sigh of relief – it was just a statue.

The statue's face looked curious. Jalby switched on his torch. In the light the man's features seemed familiar. Jalby moved closer, still half expecting the statue to leap at him. A bronze plaque adorned the pedestal and Jalby bent down so he could read it. 'Bamf Bornscale – Professor of Robotics, 2046 – 2055.' Jalby recognised the name from somewhere. It was Gorzon's father! Jalby knew that Gorzon didn't live with his father, who had separated from Gorzon's mother some years ago. Jalby hadn't heard anything else. He didn't even know Gorzon's father was a scientist. But once, Gorzon had let it slip that his father's factory in China built robots.

Jalby scanned the area. Another set of stairs curved gracefully to the floor above and he bounded up them through the gloom. He got to a heavy-looking door. His heart was thudding loudly, forcing blood round his nervous body. He pushed at the door and it swung inwards to reveal Meribrayne's untidy office. He had made it!

He was surprised how well he could see in the darkness. He could clearly make out papers and journals strewn everywhere, just as they had been the other day. Perhaps the programming had even improved their night-sight, he thought. He still needed his torch to read anything though.

Nothing of interest on the desk caught his eye. He tried the drawers. The top drawer was locked. He tried the next. It slid open easily. He fumbled around and felt a key under some papers.

'Poor security!' Jalby mumbled to himself. Within a few seconds, he had the top drawer open. More papers, but these must be more important.

He found a newspaper clipping with the headline, 'Missing boy found unharmed.' It was from a few days ago. Jalby scanned through the article. It seemed familiar – where did he know it from? Then he remembered. The hospital – the boy with no memory – it was from the day after the news broadcast. He read the story more carefully. The boy was found wandering along cliffs near the town of Shingleton. He seemed totally lost, despite living only a few miles away in the town. He was unharmed, but had no memory of how he came to be missing a month ago, or what had happened to him. There was something else unusual in the story. The boy seemed unusually obedient, and did everything that was asked of him. He even ate reconstituted porridge at the police station. His parents said they didn't recognise any of his behaviour – the last time he had done as he was told was about two years ago.

Jalby rummaged further and found a printed manuscript with technical data for the brain programmer. He leafed through it – mostly boring stuff that only Meribrayne would understand. The scientist had scribbled notes all over it in almost illegible handwriting. Jalby didn't expect to find anything in the manuscript. He was starting to wonder why he had come.

Suddenly something in the manuscript caught his eye. He lost the page, but he was sure he had seen a strange sounding word scribbled in the margin. He wasted several minutes before he found the page again. There were a few words scrawled next to a page of maths and technical data - 'zaphalod brain control.' He tried to read the printed material on the page but didn't understand any of it. Brain-programming didn't seem to help him understand brain-programming. Perhaps something on zaphalod had been programmed into his brain. He went through the school subjects in his head but he couldn't remember anything. Maybe he was trying too hard. He let the word 'zaphalod' wash over his mind – something in his brain seemed to kick into action. Then he had it for a split second – 'zaphalod – a very rare mineral which almost no one has ever seen. It originates in China...' He lost his concentration and his mind went blank. He needed more practice. It sounded ominous though – zaphalod brain control. What was Meribrayne really up to?

Jalby noticed Meribrayne's computer and tried to switch it on. No luck – it was logged off, and he didn't have the password.

He crept slowly up to the window after turning off his torch. He was amazed to see the robot still tending to Stuke. Jalby was suddenly hit with feelings of guilt. It looked as if his friend was really injured, but he could hardly go out now – and the robot knew who he was. So far, he'd hardly found out anything. He had to find something more to go on. Perhaps he'd have time to find the lab where he'd been programmed.

He made his way back to the door. The stairs outside arched upwards to the floor above. He ran up and found a long corridor stretching off into the darkness. Jalby couldn't tell how far it went. Doors led off to labs on either side of the corridor as far as he could see. Finding his lab could take forever.

He gently opened the first door and shone his torch inside. He didn't recognise anything. There were banks of computers, with hundreds of coloured lights flashing on and off, but nothing like a brain programmer to be seen. Then he remembered. The programmer was in pieces, and unlikely to have been rebuilt.

He tried several more rooms, some with chemicals flowing noisily along tubes – mysterious experiments that seemed to be going on all night. He moved stealthily along the corridor, but there was no sound except for his hurried breathing. He took a few deep breaths to try to calm his nerves.

Suddenly there was the sound of footsteps coming up a staircase ten metres further along the corridor. He could tell they weren't human. There was a slight squeaky sound as metal joints rotated, and the whirring sound of electronic processors. It was the robot, rapidly getting closer, able to see clearly in the dark.

Jalby opened the door of the nearest lab and dived in, closing the door behind him as quietly as he could. He leaned against the back of the door, desperately trying to hold his breath. He heard the robot walk past outside. He thought he heard it pause outside the door, but then it carried on.

Jalby allowed his eyes to adapt to the gloom. There was a small amount of light from a tiny window high up in the opposite wall. Again he noticed how the programming seemed to have sharpened his night vision. After a few seconds he realised he was in a storeroom, with old electrical devices piled up on metal shelving. A second door led off to the left of the room. He opened it and cursed as it screeched noisily on un-oiled hinges. Jalby paused for a moment – he seemed to remember that sound.

The next room was a large lab. He scanned the room and saw pieces of machinery scattered across it. He picked out a console that was badly smashed up. This was it – the programmer! It was in a sorry state. The force of the explosion had ripped it to shreds. He felt lucky to be alive.

Just then, he noticed light round the edges of a door at the far side of the lab. He hardly had time to think. At that moment, the door opened, flooding the room with fluorescent light. Jalby slipped underneath the bed where he had been programmed, blood thumping through his temples. His back scraped against broken glass, still on the floor after the accident.

Whoever had walked in switched the lab lights on. Even under the bed, Jalby had to shut his eyes, to protect them from the glare. As the footsteps passed to the other side of the lab, Jalby risked a quick look. It was Doctor Scorpface. What was he doing here so late? Jalby froze with fear as Scorpface made his way back towards the wrecked programmer, and the bed. Jalby tried to make himself as small as possible: he couldn't even tell if his feet were sticking out from under the edge. Scorpface passed round the bed and bent down to look at the shattered screen of the programmer. Jalby was just a metre from Scorpface's head. He could smell garlic on his breath – he wanted to gag. He was holding his breath, hoping the scientist would disappear again. Scorpface didn't seem to be going anywhere: he just seemed to be standing there, examining the smashed machine. Jalby had never held his breath for this long in his life – he thought his lungs were going to burst.

Suddenly, someone's phone went off. Jalby's heart skipped a beat. It sounded like his own phone.

'Hello sir,' Scorpface said in his whiny voice. 'I'm just looking now. It's such a mess, and the scope is smashed.'

There was a pause. Jalby could just hear someone's voice at the other end, but he couldn't tell who it was.

'The positive lead goes to the data analyser,' Scorpface continued.

'Yes, I think it will work with the zaphalod.'

Jalby's eyes widened.

Another pause. Who was Scorpface speaking to?

'But we've questioned Meribrayne. She's not giving anything away. I need a bit more time.' Scorpface was starting to sound desperate. 'Yes, ok sir – it will be ready this weekend.'

Scorpface ended the call, bent down once more to look at the innards of the programmer and then returned to the office. Jalby tried to get his breath back. Half a minute later, Scorpface walked back through the lab, switched off the lights and disappeared through the door.

Jalby didn't have a clue what was going on. Scorpface seemed to have a different boss, and they were against Meribrayne. Jalby remembered Meribrayne's scribbled words – zaphalod brain control. It didn't sound good.

The lab was once more in darkness. Jalby was losing his taste for snooping around and he wanted to leave immediately, but he still had the robot to get past. It could still be wandering the corridors, which might allow Jalby to escape through the front entrance – but if not?

He silently left the lab and felt his way along the corridor to the stairs he had seen earlier. He didn't dare use his torch, but he could just about see by the dim moonlight shining through a sky-light. He inched down the stairs and passed along several more narrow corridors which weaved through the building. There was no light now and he had no choice but to switch his torch on again.

Just then, Jalby heard the sound of robotic feet stomping quickly along a corridor. The robot was coming back! Jalby wrenched open a door and leaped through, but the robot had seen his torchlight. 'Stop where you are!' the robot bleated in its tinny voice. Jalby heard the steps quicken. He slammed the door. The robot would be there in a few seconds. What could he do? He shone his torch around what seemed to be another lab. Five metres away was a door with a sign saying 'private'. Jalby bolted through it, just as the robot burst into the lab. He heard the robot bound over to the door, but it came no further.

'Come out now. You can not escape. You are in danger,' the robot repeated several times. Jalby guessed why it didn't try to open the door. It had to follow orders, no matter what, and this room, whatever it was, was private. Jalby felt completely trapped. There were no doors or windows in the room. A wave of fatigue suddenly came over him. Perhaps he could get past the robot, just like they did on the basketball court, but he realised he could no longer see properly. Everything was hazy. He was feeling dizzy. He slumped to the floor. Something in the room was sapping his energy. He made a desperate grab for the door and collapsed.

Chapter 9

Jalby was surprised to wake up in a comfortable bed, with the sun streaming through the window. He didn't recognise the room, but it looked as if he was still somewhere in the research institute. He felt remarkably refreshed and wondered how long he'd been asleep.

Suddenly, Scorpface walked into the room and Jalby recoiled with fright.

'Relax Jalby, relax. There'll be time to explain everything.'

The robot from reception brought him some breakfast, while Scorpface disappeared from the room again. Jalby didn't feel like he was in trouble, yet he had just been caught snooping around the labs in the middle of the night. He tried to think of an excuse, but it seemed a hopeless task.

Scorpface came back a few minutes later.

'Sorry you didn't quite manage to escape last night. Unfortunately for you, you ran straight into our brainwave lab,' Scorpface said smiling. 'You were lucky. We were testing high intensity waves – strong enough to send a gorilla to sleep. You could have been killed.'

Jalby gulped.

'We were very impressed that you somehow managed to break in to the institute,' Scorpface continued. 'Perhaps you could tell us how you managed to get past our robot here – it doesn't normally miss anything. Sadly we've had to reassign its duties. It will hopefully do a better job of making tea instead.'

Jalby decided not to say anything and let Scorpface continue.

'Did you find what you were looking for?' the scientist asked.

'I just wanted a look round.'

'You went to a lot of trouble for a look round, Jalby.'

'It's an interesting place, so it was worth the trouble.'

'And you never thought to ask us first for a guided tour? We could have told you a lot more.'

Jalby shrugged. 'Sorry. Guided tours never seem to show you the best bits.'

'We're glad you're showing an interest in our work here. Most students are only interested in trendy subjects, like computer animation, never science. We couldn't get people to visit if we paid them.'

Jalby smiled to himself.

'Unfortunately, Professor Meribrayne has had to go away for a few days. Otherwise, she could have explained everything that goes on here – far better than me.'

'What have you done with Meribrayne?' Jalby demanded.

Scorpface cleared his throat.

'Meribrayne is in good hands. Why do you ask?'

'I don't believe you. You are holding her captive.'

Jalby realised he had said too much.

'Do you really think you are in a position to question me?' The scientist asked him coldly. He seemed to be weighing Jalby up – deciding if he was a threat.

'I and the other scientists have been getting a little worried about Meribrayne lately,' Scorpface said at last. 'We don't want her to ruin our experiments.'

'Aren't you all working together?' asked Jalby.

'We were,' said Scorpface firmly. 'Unfortunately, we believe that Meribrayne, for reasons of her own, would like to sabotage the project.'

'Why on earth would she want to do that?'

'We think she is becoming a little too protective. She invented brain programming, and she doesn't want anyone to interfere with it – to make it better. She wants it to be her project, and hers alone.'

Jalby stayed quiet.

'Now, perhaps Jalby you could tell me why you were running around our research institute in the middle of the night.'

'I was bored. We don't have to go to school, and I wanted something to do.'

Scorpface smiled and then suddenly moved closer.

'You were called to Meribrayne's office after the tests at school,' he said slowly.

'Ah, yes. She wanted to give me a check-up,' replied Jalby.

'Of course, of course. You do understand that I am on your side?'

Jalby nodded.

'We would not want anything to happen to you, would we?' Scorpface sounded threatening. 'You and the others are very valuable. You are the first children to have been successfully programmed by Meribrayne. Unfortunately, she has forgotten that this project is not about her – it is about helping humanity.'

Scorpface turned to the robot. 'Ok, you can bring him through now.'

A second later, Stuke limped into the room followed by the robot. He wasn't his usual lively self and avoided looking at Jalby.

'Oh, come. You're not going to pretend you had nothing to do with this escapade of Jalby's are you?' laughed Scorpface. 'Say hello to your friend.'

'Hello Jalby,' said Stuke sullenly.

Jalby tried his best to smile.

'Now, stay away from the research institute. It's for your own good. We will be in touch,' Scorpface said sternly.

The boys nodded automatically, muttering 'Yes sir,' before they were ushered out of the institute.

Back outside, Stuke's face suddenly brightened up.

'They've fixed my scooter. It was wrecked after my crash!'

They walked to the street where Jalby had parked his own scooter, while they spoke about what had happened.

'So was the crash bad?' asked Jalby.

'It was my worst ever – I think I overdid it! Those were real screams you know, and you just carried on into the building!'

'Sorry Stuke. I just thought you were good at acting. But you were in good hands, weren't you? I don't think they programmed first aid into our brains.'

'Nah, too practical. I don't think they programmed how to win at computer games either.'

'So how come you ended up staying the night? Were they good hosts?'

'Well, I did my leg in a bit. Really neat stitches that robot made, look,' Stuke pulled up his trouser leg to show what looked like it had been a nasty gash from the night before.

'But I think the robot got suspicious. It went back for a few seconds. I was limping away with my scooter. Then it came jumping out again and arrested me. Perhaps it was the security stuff not working that made it suspect me. Anyway, the robot dragged me inside and locked me in a room.'

'When did Scorpface come along?'

'That was an hour later,' Stuke replied.

'Did you…' Jalby started asking.

'They'd already found you: I didn't give you away,' said Stuke hurriedly.

'And did Scorpface question you? Did you tell him anything?'

'We don't have much to tell. He kept asking why we were here. I just said we were looking around. He didn't seem to believe me. After a bit, he must have thought he wouldn't get anywhere and he gave up.'

'Do you trust him?' asked Jalby.

'It sounds possible. Meribrayne could be up to no good. What about you?'

'I don't know. I don't think I trust any of them at the moment – this zaphalod business doesn't sound good.'

They got to Jalby's scooter and flew back into the town centre. Jalby was dreading going back to his aunt's - he hadn't expected to be out all night. He picked up his phone and called home, holding the handset at arm's length.

'Jalby, it's you! I ought to stop you going out for a month,' his aunt began. That 'ought to' didn't sound as bad as it could have done.

'Sorry auntie, Stuke had an accident.'

'Yes, I know. You were out riding again, weren't you? I don't trust you on those awful scooters. As you rescued your friend, I shall overlook it this time – however, next time you sneak out late, I'll ground you for a month. Do you understand?'

'Yes auntie, bye auntie.'

Jalby was wondering what Scorpface had told her. Whatever it was, he had escaped lightly.

'Did you hear that?' he asked Stuke.

'Of course I heard it. It was your aunt.'

He had a point. It was amazing Malinka didn't burst the speaker, the way she bellowed down the phone.

'So you rescued me did you?' asked Stuke sarcastically.

'Something like that. So what now? Any ideas?'

'How about we go back to the arcade, and you can test your gaming skills?' suggested Stuke enthusiastically.

'I was thinking of something in the real world.'

'Like what? I don't see how we can do anything, except stay out of trouble. Might as well enjoy ourselves, before anyone realises we've got nothing to do.'

'I think we should head back to school,' Jalby said.

'Are you serious?' Stuke asked in amazement. 'We go to all this trouble to have our brains programmed, and you want to go back to school!'

Jalby told Stuke about the statue he had stumbled upon.

'I want to find out what Gorzon's father did at the institute.'

'Right, so we just go ahead and ask the scariest kid in the school if his dad is mixed up in all this!' Stuke said, rolling his eyes.

'You can ask him if you like, but I've got a better idea,' Jalby replied as they flew off towards school.

Chapter 10

They parked their scooters a few hundred metres from the school and walked quickly to the back entrance. As they approached, the school seemed silent.

'Must all be studying hard. They know they've got a lot of work to do to catch up with us,' said Stuke.

'They'll be there for a long time,' replied Jalby. 'Anyway, here's what we're going to do.'

It was soon going to be physical education, and Jalby thought this would be a good time for some research. He explained his plan to Stuke.

'So we wait until they've left the changing rooms, head in to find Gorzon's phone – then we can download his messages.'

'Got you,' replied Stuke.

They hid behind a large palm tree, out of sight of the main school buildings. Several minutes later the noise levels built up. Jalby guessed they were leaving the classrooms to get changed. Soon they heard the doors bang open and a stream of children came running out, pushing each other and screaming. It was as if they hadn't been allowed out the building for weeks.

Jalby looked round and caught sight of Lara offering a sick note to Mr Gutborg, the games teacher for the afternoon. No change there, Jalby thought. Lara would spend the entire class texting her friend from another school, who would also have a sick note so she wouldn't have to do any sport either.

They waited a few more minutes for everyone to disappear onto the football pitch.

'Ok, let's go in,' said Jalby quietly.

They headed for a little-used side door. Jalby pressed his thumb against the door lock and waited for the iris scan. The door beeped but nothing happened.

'It doesn't recognise my iris. You try!'

Stuke gave it a go and again it didn't work.

'Nice to know we're still welcome,' he said.

Suddenly Jalby pushed Stuke back against the wall. Someone was coming towards the door. A moment later, Lara left the building. She was so busy texting, she walked straight past, oblivious to them. Stuke made a face, as if to say 'that was close,' and they hurried inside before the door closed automatically. They tiptoed along a corridor, down some steps, and then headed for the boys' changing room.

'Right, you look along that wall and I'll try this one,' Jalby ordered.

After a few seconds, Stuke found Gorzon's uniform. It was far bigger than anyone else's, except for those of his two friends, Smoyd and Dorf.

'I've got it!' Stuke called over.

They found Gorzon's phone and linked it to Jalby's phone.

'Right, it'll just take a few seconds to copy across his files and messages.'

'Good job Gorzon doesn't have the sense to have a password,' observed Stuke.

A few seconds later a message appeared on Jalby's screen – 'Download complete.'

He carefully replaced Gorzon's phone and they headed back to the door.

'That was dead easy!' remarked Stuke.

'Too easy,' said Jalby.

A second later, Mr Prodorg came round the corner and stood staring at them as if they were aliens.

'Well, look who it is!' he said finally. 'Have you been missing school? How nice of you to come back and pay us a visit!'

The words seemed friendly, but there was a hint of malice in Prodorg's voice. He probably hadn't forgotten his crash with Stuke's scooter only a few days earlier, and Jalby noticed a long scratch on his face that they hadn't seen before.

'So, any particular reason why you decided to drop by?'

'Err. We thought we'd drop by because it's sports afternoon. Course, we're normally kept really busy,' said Stuke quickly.

'Is that so? Well, you don't look dressed for sports, but I don't think that'll be a problem. I see you've dispensed with the school uniform already.'

The school uniform was a horrible green and brown colour. Like other clothes, it was a single layer, but it was so itchy everyone hated it. Stuke had burned his the day after he had got his results.

Prodorg limped as he led them back outside to the playing fields. They saw Mr Gutborg trying to control something that only vaguely resembled a football match. Gutborg was lolloping across the pitch, panting and wheezing. Ten children were chasing after the ball, and no-one seemed to understand the concept of positioning.

Prodorg started to smile when he spotted Gorzon, Dorf and

Smoyd, all on the same side. Jalby and Stuke exchanged worried glances.

They guessed which team was winning. Whenever Gorzon had the ball, which was often, everyone seemed to keep a respectable distance from him.

As they got closer, they were amazed to see Talia playing for the other team.

'What's Talia doing here?' Stuke blurted out.

'Probably the same reason you're here, remember. Perhaps, for some inexplicable reason, she too was missing school,' replied Mr Prodorg dryly.

'Oh yeah,' said Stuke. 'Hey, she's doing well!'

She had got control of the ball and skilfully weaved it past Gorzon. She didn't consider passing, but passing wasn't normal in a game of school football.

'She's nearly at the goal. And she scores!' yelled Stuke.

Her team cheered loudly and patted her on her back.

'She's always been a good player,' said Jalby.

'Looks like she's even better now!' enthused Stuke.

Jalby remembered how Talia used to dispatch players with

frightening regularity if they got in her way. Her tackles seemed far less vicious now – she was one of the more elegant players on the pitch.

Mr Prodorg called Mr Gutborg over and a moment later Jalby had left his bag with his phone at the side of the pitch, hoping no-one would tread on it, or use it as target practice with the ball.

'Ok, you on that side and you over there,' Mr Gutborg bellowed above the shouting, as the players saw who was joining them. Jalby found himself on the same team as Talia, while Stuke unwillingly trudged over to the opposition, with Gorzon scowling at him.

Within a few seconds, Gorzon had tried running straight at Jalby, even though Jalby didn't actually have the ball. Jalby stepped out the way and Gorzon staggered past harmlessly. Soon Stuke had the ball and was flying down the pitch towards the goal. He hadn't reckoned on Talia. She tackled him skilfully and took possession. She ignored the other players on her team and passed to Jalby. Jalby weaved past Smoyd, who looked like he was about to start playing rugby. Another few paces and Jalby planted the ball in the corner of the net. The goalkeeper looked as if something supersonic had caught him unawares. Gorzon was clenching his fists and scowling more than ever, especially after Jalby flashed him a broad smile.

The game carried on. Jalby tried a brave tackle on Dorf, but Smoyd came up behind, swiping his legs from under him.

'Referee! Did you see that!?' someone yelled. Clearly Mr Gutborg hadn't seen anything –he only seemed to see the ball and whoever was attached to it.

Dorf was struggling after running only halfway across the pitch. He actually passed the ball to a team-mate, who was tackled by Talia. Stuke came in to help his team-mate and took the ball from Talia. He sprinted towards the goal, more quickly than anyone else on the pitch, left several defenders standing, and scored. His team started shouting 'Stuke! Stuke!', except for Gorzon, who seemed as angry as ever.

Soon the tables had turned. Jalby and Talia had each scored another goal, almost without even trying. Their team-mates looked on amazed. Jalby was usually about as good at football as he had been at basketball.

Mr Gutborg looked more tired than anyone when he finally blew the whistle – he was hunched over so much his nose was nearly touching the muddy ground. Jalby's team cheered noisily – they had expected to lose badly, with Gorzon and his friends on the other side. They saw Gorzon heading from the pitch, arguing with Smoyd and Dorf.

Jalby went over to speak to Talia, who was seeing how long she could keep the ball in the air.

'Seven, eight, nine... Oops, sorry sir!'

The ball whacked Mr Gutborg on the back of his head as he was heading off the pitch. He stumbled and carried on staggering towards the school.

'Showing off again!' Stuke said.

'Shut up!' shouted Talia.

'Notice anything different about how you're playing football?' asked Jalby.

'Yeah, I seem to have improved a lot since I last played. I haven't even been practising.'

'It's the brain programming. It improves our coordination,' explained Jalby.

Talia looked taken aback, but then disappointed. 'You mean I wouldn't play like this if I hadn't been programmed?'

'Nope. Afraid not. It really helped our basketball too.'

'But you can't even play basketball!'

'Exactly!' Jalby smiled. 'Listen, we need to talk about the programming. Something weird has been going on.'

Jalby told her about the zaphalod and their visit to the lab in the night.

'Wow, you've been busy. So someone's up to no good,' Talia said.

'That's what it sounds like,' Jalby replied.

They left the school before he took out his phone. 'I've downloaded messages and everything from Gorzon's phone. I found out his father used to work at the lab – perhaps he's behind it all.'

'Gorzon's never even mentioned his dad. Do you really think he talks to his dad about this stuff?' Talia asked.

'I don't know, but it's worth trying. It might give us a few clues.'

Jalby took out his phone and started trawling through Gorzon's messages. 'Here's one from his mother.'

'Does she tell him not to be late home from school?' Stuke asked.

'Stuke, try to be serious for once in your life,' said Talia.

Jalby opened up a dozen more, but found nothing important. He was starting to feel guilty. They were spying on Gorzon for no reason. Of course he didn't know anything about it – he was just a child, like them. Jalby opened another message.

110

'Wait a minute, look at this!'

He read out the message: 'Gorzon, we have something which may help you. Meet me at Kraston Park at eight on Friday. Come alone, Scorpface.'

'Why's Gorzon in touch with Scorpface?' asked Talia.

'Who knows? What do we do now? It doesn't tell us much,' said Stuke.

'I'm going to that park on Friday,' said Jalby.

'Then I'm coming too, just in case you get discovered and we never see you again.'

'How touching, Stuke,' said Talia. 'I suppose I'll just hang around and do some research. I'll try to track down Bort and Dana.'

'Good thinking Talia.' Stuke was looking at her as if to say 'We can manage without you.'

'Don't patronise me! You think that I can't look after myself.'

'We know you can look after yourself – we've seen you play football,' replied Jalby. 'You can come if you like - but we're probably more likely to be seen if we all go to the park.'

Talia turned on her heels and strode off.

'Good to have another team member on the case. We can crack this in no time,' said Stuke.

Jalby didn't look quite so convinced.

Chapter 11

It was a long wait for Friday evening. Jalby and Stuke had seen nothing of Talia and decided to leave her to her own detective work.

It was nearly eight. Even though the park was in the outskirts of the city, it seemed a long way from civilisation. It was the perfect place to meet secretly.

They had already crept in through a side entrance of the park. The park was lit only by moonlight, and trees were casting mysterious shadows across the narrow paths. Branches creaked noisily in the breeze. Once, they thought they saw people ahead of them, but they were just old tree stumps. Jalby shivered, even though he wasn't cold.

They made their way slowly towards the main entrance, as close as they dared. Suddenly a heavily built figure shuffled through the half-closed gate. It was Gorzon, dressed all in black.

'Get down,' whispered Jalby. They crawled through long grass and hid behind a large tree.

At eight on the dot Scorpface appeared from nowhere and walked behind Gorzon. They saw Gorzon jump in surprise.

'Not normal to see Gorzon so nervous,' whispered Stuke.

'I'm going to get closer so I can hear,' said Jalby, before creeping away through dense trees and bushes. He got within ten metres before Gorzon and Scorpface set off walking slowly into the park. Jalby cursed under his breath as they moved further away. He followed behind and tried to record their conversation with the microphone on his phone.

'It's, it's a strange place to meet, Scorpface. Why here?' asked Gorzon suspiciously.

'Well, we can't have the authorities knowing we are attempting to program a sixth person, can we?' Scorpface replied.

'Have you figured out how to program me?' Gorzon asked hopefully.

'I'm afraid not. It's proving a difficult problem.'

Gorzon looked disappointed.

'I don't understand why it won't work for me,' he replied gruffly.

'Well, to put it simply, your brain seems to be wired up slightly differently. When we did tests, we found that your brain wouldn't retain any of the knowledge we programmed in.'

'So, does this mean I have no choice but to go to school, even though my father helped to develop brain programming?'

'I'm afraid so Gorzon. There's nothing that can be done. Except…'

'Except what?'

'You remember Professor Dolgov, who worked with your father and Professor Meribrayne.'

'Yes.'

'During the development of the technique, Dolgov found something which could make brain programming even more powerful than it already is.'

They walked within a few metres of Stuke, or where Jalby thought Stuke was. It was difficult to tell in the gloom. Jalby tried to follow them as quietly as he could, freezing whenever a twig cracked beneath his weight.

'Unknown to Meribrayne, Dolgov came across a very rare substance called zaphalod some years ago. This material had a very curious effect on the programming.'

'How can this help me?' asked Gorzon.

'If you help us Gorzon, we'll help you. You can help us find out why your brain was unsuitable for programming. Then we might find a way…'

'But what does this zaphalod do?'

'Zaphalod means we can control what a child does, so they never do anything wrong or get into trouble.'

'What, so we become like robots?' Gorzon sneered.

Jalby thought of the boy walking along the south coast – unharmed but without a memory, and a lot more obedient than any normal child.

Gorzon seemed to have heard the news too:

'Was that boy on the TV turned into a robot?'

'Not exactly,' explained Scorpface. 'You see, Dolgov hadn't yet perfected brain programming. This child was an early experiment, along with several others. These children are obedient, but they can't be made to do very much.'

'That boy has lost his memory. You don't have a clue what you're doing!' Gorzon snapped.

'On the contrary, we've got it all worked out, now that Professor Meribrayne has successfully shown us how to program children properly. It's just a shame she doesn't approve,' Scorpface said darkly. 'Right now, one of the five children who were programmed by Meribrayne is going to Dolgov's underground lab on the south coast. This child has the zaphalod added to the microchip in their brain, and they will start the process of being turned into a human robot. Then we will see how we can help you, Gorzon.'

'I'm not having anything to do with your research. You're not telling me what to do!'

'We wouldn't want you to be left out, would we?' Scorpface said slyly. 'When we finally work out how to program you, you will be allowed special privileges for helping us. The programming will make you even stronger than you are now, and you will be able to control other programmed children.'

'But I will be a robot, working for you!' Gorzon hissed.

'An unfortunate attitude, but one which I had predicted. People just don't seem to realise how useful this could all be to society. Not even your father understood its importance.'

'My father would never have turned anyone into a robot, and if he was still around he'd make sure you wouldn't as well.'

'Gorzon, since when have you been so moralistic? I thought you wanted us to help you?'

'I just wanted to be programmed like the others!'

'You're just as stubborn as your father was. If he had gone along with Dolgov's plan to use zaphalod, things might have been different – he could have been part of this great project.'

'How convenient for you that my father died in that accident.'

Gorzon was scowling and inching closer to the scientist, clenching his massive fists. Normally people didn't hang around to see what Gorzon would do next, especially if they were as puny-looking as Scorpface. But Scorpface stood his ground.

'What are you suggesting Gorzon? That we somehow arranged the accident? That would be quite an accusation. Unfortunately, now Professor Meribrayne has discovered our plans for zaphalod she too seems to be a little reluctant to take part...'

Scorpface got no further. Gorzon lunged at him with all his might, but the scientist stepped out of the way shouting 'Now!'

Suddenly the undergrowth parted and Jalby watched a huge robot leap forward with amazing speed. A second later, the robot had grabbed Gorzon round the neck and lifted him clean off the ground, effortlessly. At any other time Jalby would have enjoyed seeing this happen to Gorzon, but right now he actually felt he should be doing something to help. He looked round and saw Stuke creeping up behind him. They both looked on helplessly.

'Ok, be careful with him,' Scorpface commanded the robot. 'He's going to be very useful to Dolgov.'

'I'm not helping you to do anything!' Gorzon spat.

'It doesn't look like you have much choice, does it?' Scorpface

118

said with a sneer. 'Load him on!'

The robot dragged Gorzon into the bushes, dropped him in the luggage compartment of a large scooter and locked the lid. A second later, Scorpface jumped onto a second scooter and they roared off into the night.

Jalby and Stuke looked at each other dumbfounded. Neither spoke until the scooters had disappeared.

'I can't believe it!' said Stuke finally. 'What are we going to do?'

Jalby kept looking up to where the scooters had gone.

'I don't know. The police won't listen. We can't even contact Meribrayne.'

'Perhaps Talia's found out something,' suggested Stuke. 'Let's go and find her.'

Jalby remembered what Scorpface had told Gorzon.

'Perhaps she's found out who has the zaphalod. Scorpface said one of us has it, and this person is heading to his lab on the south coast.'

'Well, sounds like we're safe. Can't say I've got any sudden desire to lose my freedom,' said Stuke.

They rode their scooters back into town, weaving in and out of heavy traffic as they neared the centre.

Talia lived in one of the new towers, in an apartment on the two-hundred-and-thirty-fifth floor, almost a kilometre high. She claimed she always went up the stairs, to keep fit, unless she was in a real hurry. Jalby and Stuke took the lift.

'Ten storeys a second, this lift. Shame we can't ride up from outside though,' Stuke remarked.

'We could, but that would be a bit obvious.'

Adults could actually fly to the top of high buildings, but children were limited to the ground, as usual. Jalby didn't think it was a good idea to push their luck on their modified scooters.

A minute later they were standing outside Talia's front door, while a camera watched them and scanned their irises. The door slid open slowly, as if it was still deciding whether it liked the look of them. A tall, elegant-looking robot ushered them inside.

'Didn't know she had a butler,' Stuke whispered.

'We can only afford our robot dog, and it's hopeless at doing anything,' complained Jalby. 'The last time it blew up the reconstitutor, my auntie decided to keep it outside on the balcony.'

They were taken through to a vast lounge with a sofa longer than

Jalby's flat.

'Well, look who it is!' Talia announced as she strode into the room. 'My parents are out, so make yourselves at home.'

The boys collapsed on the sofa, but jumped up a second later when a wave of water appeared out of nowhere, heading straight for them. Talia laughed.

'Do you like our virtual lounge?' she asked.

A three dimensional image of the sea and sky appeared before their eyes. They watched as smaller waves started lapping at their feet. They looked identical to real waves, but their feet didn't get wet.

'Very clever,' said Stuke as he sat down again. 'I thought we were going to drown!'

They looked out over a tropical bay, listening to exotic birds which seemed to be flying round the room. The sofa appeared to be at the edge of a beautiful white beach, with palm trees swaying in a gentle breeze.

A few seconds later, the robot came back with a tray of drinks.

'That was a good guess – I really needed some borg juice,' said Jalby.

'And it got me my favourite – Marv's Mango,' said Stuke.

'It wasn't a guess,' said Talia proudly. 'Our robot can read the signals in your brain, and bring you whatever you want to eat or drink.'

'Wow, does it read all of your thoughts?' asked Stuke.

'Not yet, but they're working on an upgrade – who knows what that will be able to do.'

Jalby explained what had happened since they had last spoken.

'So basically Scorpface and this scientist Dolgov are against Meribrayne and one of us is going to be turned into a human robot – the person who has the zaphalod. And they're going to try to program Gorzon,' said Talia.

'That's about right. We don't know who has the zaphalod, but we don't feel like there's anything weird going on in our brains. Did you find out anything?' asked Jalby.

'I tracked down Bort and he seems fine. Spoke to him earlier. He doesn't feel any different from before the programming. But he says he's even better at basketball.'

'He didn't feel like leaving home to become a slave to a mad scientist?' asked Stuke.

'Sorry, I didn't know to ask. But Dana…'

'What about Dana?' asked Jalby.

'Well, I did some investigating and found out where she lives. I called for her yesterday. Her mother answered, but Dana wasn't in. Apparently, she's been behaving a bit weirdly since the programming. Her mother seems quite worried.'

'What, is she more weird than normal?' Stuke asked.

'She's even quieter than usual, really quiet, doesn't say where she's going, just disappears for the day. Her mother asked if we'd had any side effects after the programming.'

'I don't think it would make much difference to Dana if she was turned into a robot.'

'Stuke, she's normally alright! Just takes a while to get to know her,' Talia said.

They were quiet for a moment. Suddenly the TV seemed to switch itself on. Talia could control it with her mind, much to Jalby's surprise – his aunt's TV still had a remote control, with flat batteries.

The news was coming to an end and Stuke was getting excited.

'That reality TV show will be on next – it's getting good. They really do think they've been transported back in time to 2000.'

'Stuke listen!' Talia said.

The closing story had them glued to the screen. They moved to within a few metres of the TV, even though it was two metres wide.

'That's... Dana!' cried Talia.

The newscaster sounded even more serious than usual – 'The girl was reported missing this morning after not returning home last night, and after her parents failed to contact her on her phone. Her mother reported that before she disappeared, she seemed distracted and almost incapable of making conversation. The security services are urging anyone with any information to come forward.'

The news ended and the three sat there, stunned. Stuke was the first to speak.

'So, they've got Dana. I think we should go to the police.'

Talia was sceptical.

'They'd never believe us. Dolgov and Scorpface probably have friends in the police. Besides, we've got no real evidence of anything. It would be us against them,' she said.

'Hold on. Perhaps it's not too late to save her,' said Jalby. 'Scorpface said that it's a process. That means it might take time to turn her into a robot.'

'What I don't understand is how they can turn other people into robots,' said Talia. 'I mean, if they only have the zaphalod in one person, and it's so rare...'

'If she's going to be the only one, they may as well have her,' Stuke suggested casually.

Jalby thought he was joking – at least he hoped he was – but Talia didn't seem to see the funny side.

'What? How would you like to be turned into a robot?' she blurted out.

'I wouldn't like to be a robot, but she might,' Stuke replied, trying to wind Talia up even more. Talia scowled at him.

'Maybe they're looking for more of the stuff,' said Jalby. 'And when they find it, Gorzon will be next.'

'This place – the underground lab – have you any idea where it is, Jalby?' asked Stuke.

'I'm willing to bet it's near the town on the coast where the boy was found. What's it called – Shingleton.'

'Let's check it out on the Internet,' said Talia.

A moment later, a web page appeared on the TV screen, without Talia appearing to do anything.

'Nothing much here – just some boring old town by the sea, population 23,465,' said Stuke.

'Wait a minute,' said Jalby. He was struggling to remember something. 'There are cliffs a few miles along the coast. The caves in the cliffs were used for centuries by smugglers. The caves were also used during the Second World War as an underground fort.'

'And then they were used as a secret base during the Cold War, before they were closed in 1985. No-one has been allowed in them since then,' continued Talia.

'Hey, I know that, too. But I don't remember studying that in history,' said Stuke.

'It must be the programming. You never learned anything in history lessons,' joked Jalby.

'So according to what we've been programmed, no-one has been inside the caves for 75 years,' said Talia.

'My brain is telling me they're two miles west of Shingleton,' said Stuke.

'Mine too,' said Jalby. 'Can you bring up a map of the area Talia?'

A large map appeared on screen and zoomed in on the coast near the town.

'That's just as my brain told me, too,' said Jalby. 'There's a rocky peninsula, and high cliffs. No sign of any caves though.'

'Are we sure that's where Dana has gone?' asked Stuke.

Jalby thought for a moment. 'Well, we're going on what Scorpface told Gorzon. Sounds like a good place for a secret research lab.'

'But we don't even have a clue how to get in!' said Stuke.

'That's something we'll have to figure out when we get there.' Jalby said.

He remembered the boy who had been found nearby.

'Talia, are there any news reports?'

She brought up a series of stories, and they started to scan the headlines.

'Right, so here's the one about the boy. Nothing new there,' said Jalby.

'What's that one there, about the scientist?' asked Stuke.

'It's from a few years back,' said Talia. 'The body of a scientist was found floating in the sea, near the cliffs. It was Bamf Bornscale – Professor of Robotics, Gorzon's father!'

'So he was probably pushed from the cliffs!' said Stuke.

'Obviously,' said Talia. 'That way, it looked like an accident, or suicide.'

They continued scanning the reports until another story caught their eye.

'Look at this!' said Talia. 'Apparently there are no animals living on the peninsula or the cliffs. There aren't even any birds, and no-one seems to know why.'

'So murders, mad scientists, and it's practically dead,' said Stuke. 'We go to all the nicest places.'

Chapter 12

'What do you mean "he's got to go off for a few days"?' Jalby's aunt was spitting down the phone.

Unknown to her, she was speaking to Jalby. Jalby was speaking through Anton's voice-transformer, which made him sound like a woman, who was about forty years older. Jalby's aunt thought she was speaking to Professor Meribrayne. Anton had programmed the voice transformer so that you could sound like anybody you wanted to be. It was his way of bunking off school – by pretending to be his mother ringing to say that he was ill.

'He and the others just need to be tested at the lab...' Jalby tried to continue.

'I don't think I should allow him anywhere near you or your lab after what happened. And I'll tell you something else – the authorities are investigating you and this rubbish about them helping with your research. I'll make sure these children never go near you ever again!' Malinka screeched.

It wasn't looking good. Jalby's plans to escape were turning to dust. He had to think quickly. He remembered that Scorpface had spoken to his aunt only a few days before – perhaps that was the answer.

'Just one moment please Mrs Malis, I think Doctor Scorpface would like to speak to you.'

Jalby gestured frantically to Anton. Anton was sitting with his hands behind his head, enjoying the show. He suddenly realised he had to do something. He lurched forward and adjusted the transformer. A few seconds later he gave Jalby the thumbs up.

'Ah hello Mrs Malis, lovely to speak to you again,' Jalby said in the voice of a middle-aged man.

'And you Doctor. I really didn't think I'd have the pleasure again so soon. I must say though, I don't remember you having such a deep voice,' Malinka purred.

Jalby shook his head and shoved his fingers down his throat while Anton made him sound slightly higher-pitched.

'Mrs Malis, as you know, your nephew is helping us with some very important research. I would be extremely grateful if you would allow him to spend some more time with us here.'

There was a long pause. Jalby held his breath.

'Well I suppose just a few days wouldn't hurt,' Malinka said brightly. 'Just make sure he doesn't get up to anything he shouldn't, and if you need me for anything, don't hesitate to give me a call.'

'Of course Mrs Malis, goodbye,' Jalby replied hurriedly, not quite believing the sudden transformation in his aunt.

'Nice work Jalby. Now for Talia and Stuke's parents,' Anton said, rubbing his hands as his friend replaced the handset.

Jalby rehearsed the script again, before picking the phone up. He was starting to sweat.

'Good morning Mrs Klington. This is Professor Meribrayne from the research institute.'

Talia's mother seemed suspicious when Jalby stumbled over his words a few times.

'Yes, Mrs Klington. T, T, Talia will be looked well, well looked after,' he stammered.

It was probably a case of nerves which caused Jalby to accidentally knock a switch on the transformer a moment later. Suddenly the power failed and it was a few seconds before he realised he was sounding like himself again – a 12-year-old schoolboy. Anton's eyes widened in horror as he too realised what had happened.

'Are you okay, Professor Meribrayne?' Talia's mother enquired. 'You're sounding a little off today...'

Anton flicked the transformer back on faster than he had ever done anything in his life.

'Yes, I'm quite okay thank you – just got a bug in my, er, throat,' Jalby croaked, while needlessly trying to sound feminine.

'Phew. I think we got away with it!' he said, after he had slammed down the phone.

A few minutes later, Jalby had recovered enough to call Stuke's parents.

'Relax Jalby. I don't think Stuke's parents know where he is half the time,' said Anton reassuringly.

When he had finished, Jalby gave Stuke and Talia a call. They were out buying provisions for the journey ahead of them, hoping they wouldn't run out of pocket money.

'We've got enough high energy bars for a week,' Stuke told him. 'I could use one now – I'm exhausted from all this shopping.'

Jalby got up to leave Anton's flat.

'Good luck Jalby. Let me know if you run into any trouble,' Anton said outside as Jalby jumped onto his scooter.

'I will Anton. Might need you to make me sound like Meribrayne again – or perhaps someone else!'

A few hours later Jalby had gone home, packed, and fended off a dozen questions from his aunt. She had been particularly curious about Scorpface.

Jalby arrived at the rendezvous, outside the town hall. He was a few minutes early, so he checked the route again on his phone and the navigation system on his scooter.

Jalby recognised the whine of Stuke's scooter as it drew closer. With practice, he found he could tell all his friends' scooters apart. Talia followed closely behind.

'All set Jalby? How long do you reckon it'll take to get to Shingleton?' Stuke asked.

'A few hours I should think, then we'll stop and get our bearings. We should try to get to the peninsula before night - I want to see the place before it gets too dark.'

'Here, I've got us all night glasses – I reckon we might need them tonight,' Talia said. 'They're the latest model. They don't even need batteries.'

'And they look pretty cool too. Thanks Talia,' said Stuke.

Jalby had never even seen a pair of night glasses before. He looked at them suspiciously. 'Do they work?' he asked.

'Of course they do. They're brilliant. You can see even if there's no moon.'

They kept a steady pace through town so they wouldn't draw attention to themselves. Beyond the ring road, the traffic disappeared – as if the city's inhabitants were scared to leave the metropolis.

Soon, all their scooters were on auto-pilot as they cruised south along the deserted route. They fell silent and Stuke started playing a computer game on his phone.

Jalby switched on the stereo implanted in his ears and tried to relax with some music. He looked round at the impenetrable forest they were passing through. The trees were engineered to grow to their full height in only two years and crowded the road on both sides, shutting out the bright sun – it seemed almost like night-time in the forest.

Jalby glanced across at Talia. She was sleeping as her scooter steered itself onwards, but it seemed a troubled sleep. She was twisting her head from side to side, even though her scooter flew smoothly through the air.

Five minutes later and Stuke had also fallen asleep. 'Just me now,' thought Jalby. He couldn't sleep – he had too many things on his mind. He realised they didn't have any sort of plan once they arrived. Secretly he thought things were not looking good. Meribrayne had disappeared and they were on their own.

The forest was creepy, and Jalby had the feeling they were being watched as they got closer to the coast. Someone somewhere could tell exactly where they were from the signals given out by their phones. He had also heard reports about animals being fitted with tiny cameras, trained to keep watch on people. Uncle Benton told him it was the government's way of stopping people doing things they shouldn't. Several times, birds seemed to fly past from the trees, closer than usual, too close for comfort, making Jalby jump nervously.

They arrived at Shingleton by mid-afternoon. Jalby was relieved to see more signs of life again. It seemed a normal coastal town, with people milling around and scooters everywhere. They probably had no idea Dolgov's lab was only a few kilometres along the coast, conducting strange experiments.

They stopped to have a quick drink at a small café next to the sea. A boy served them without even speaking. He was about sixteen years old and had a blank expression on his face. His eyes seemed glazed over, as if he wasn't actually aware of anything.

'Look at the boy behind the counter,' Jalby whispered to Talia and Stuke, as the boy disappeared to pick up a bottle of orange juice. 'Notice anything strange?'

'Come on, let's hurry up,' Talia said. 'This place seems weird somehow – there's something wrong.'

'You're just imagining things,' said Stuke. 'He's just bored of working here and bored of this town. You're letting all this stuff get to you.'

'Perhaps,' said Jalby uncertainly. They finished their drinks quickly. 'Anyway, we'll leave you with your new friend. I'm off.'

'Me too,' said Talia.

Stuke looked back at the boy and decided he wasn't going to be left behind.

'Alright, I'm coming. Let's go and find Dana.'

As they left the café, Stuke walked straight into a girl outside.

'Oops, sorry!' Stuke blurted out. The girl appeared not to even notice, but carried on walking, with the same blank expression as the boy in the café.

'Come on. Let's get out of here,' said Stuke.

Talia started to look concerned as they headed back to their scooters.

'You ok Talia?' Jalby asked.

'I don't know. How many of them are there?'

'How many what?' asked Stuke.

'Those children. Do you think Dolgov experimented on them, and they don't even know who they are anymore?'

They passed more children in the street. Many of them seemed to have the same expressionless faces.

'Is there nothing anyone can do to help them?' Talia continued.

'I don't see what we can do,' said Stuke. 'It's not as if we can just deprogram them.'

'We need to think about Dana first, otherwise she will be next,' Jalby said.

They could see the cliffs in the distance, towering over the sea. The cliffs didn't seem any closer when they reached the edge of the town. Talia suddenly realised they had a problem.

'Of course, how stupid of me!' she said. 'You didn't finish adapting my scooter, Stuke. It won't allow me to go any further. We're not on an official route.'

'Looks like you're walking then,' replied Stuke, with a broad smile.

'If I'm walking then you're walking too!' Talia shouted.

'Come on Talia, get on the back of mine,' Stuke suggested.

'I'd rather walk – you ride like a lunatic.'

'Get on the back of mine then,' said Jalby.

They set off over a dusty track that followed the coastline, with Talia clinging to the back of Jalby's scooter.

'Slow down Stuke, I can't keep up,' Jalby shouted.

Soon they lost the track and were flying over tree-tops one second and the beach the next. They made good progress for a while, but then the weather changed. Clear skies gave way to dark, menacing clouds.

'Where did this weather come from?' asked Stuke. 'It's weird, I've never known it to change this quickly.'

Above the trees, the wind had picked up so much it was nearly blowing them off their scooters.

'Jalby, let's go down, I can't hold on like this,' said Talia.

They dropped to the forest floor, where they were at least sheltered from the gale.

'This is going to get really slow,' moaned Stuke. 'Look at how thick the forest is!'

Their scooters crept onwards through the trees as dense branches tugged at their clothes.

'We could try to get back to the coast and follow the beach, but it's more sheltered here at least,' said Jalby.

The afternoon was drawing on towards dusk and it was rapidly getting dark in the forest.

'This is no good,' said Jalby at last.

He studied the screen on his scooter's navigation system. 'We're better walking. We've only got another two kilometres to go.'

Jalby's scooter descended and landed softly on the forest floor and Stuke followed after almost colliding with a tree.

'It's going to be quieter this way as well. They may have their spies.'

As Jalby said this, Stuke yelled. A pair of wings flapped furiously overhead.

'Relax, it was just a bird,' said Jalby.

'I thought we read that nothing lives here?' replied Talia. 'I'm getting my night glasses out. I'd feel happier knowing what we're heading into.'

'Are you sure?' Stuke asked nervously. 'By the way, Jalby, I thought you said we could see more clearly at night!'

'We can, to a point. But not in complete darkness.'

Their night glasses cut through the pitch black of the forest as they scrambled on.

'Wish I knew about these when I was at the lab that night,' said Jalby.

After a while, the trees started to thin out and become more spindly. 'We must be getting close now, surely,' said Stuke.

'Shh!' hissed Talia. 'Did you hear something?' she whispered.

They stopped and listened to the wind in the branches.

'It's nothing. Just the storm,' said Stuke, as if trying to convince himself. 'Nothing to worry about.'

Suddenly, they snatched a snippet of conversation through the trees. They crouched close to the ground and held their breaths as whoever it was got closer. Two figures were approaching just metres away. They were shining a torch around as they stumbled clumsily through the trees. They were heading in roughly the same direction, but seemed to be arguing about where they were going.

'The navigator is wrong, I'm telling you!'

Jalby recognised the voice immediately. After they'd passed, he turned to Talia and Stuke.

'Dorf!' he whispered, 'and Smoyd.'

'Gorzon's side-kicks have come to rescue him!' whispered back Stuke.

'Let's follow them, slowly. They seem to be heading more or less in the right direction,' said Jalby.

'Are you sure? Check your phone,' said Talia.

The map on his phone seemed to be going wrong. It was showing several different bearings, before dissolving on the screen. It didn't seem to show where they were, or where they were going to.

'It's useless,' said Jalby finally. 'It's not working properly. I think we should see where they go to.'

They followed twenty metres behind, watching Dorf's torch-light.

'Quite easy to follow when they're lit up like a Christmas tree,' said Stuke.

The branches started getting thicker again, and they scratched their faces as they fought their way through. Dorf and Smoyd suddenly seemed to have stopped.

'Did you hear something?' they thought they heard Dorf ask.

Dorf started moving again. He seemed to be retracing his steps, back towards Jalby and the others. Jalby thought they were going to be discovered. The wind picked up even more and started howling ferociously through the trees. They saw Dorf's torch shine upwards and then go out. Suddenly, Dorf and Smoyd were no longer there. It was as if they'd been dreaming them.

Jalby could feel his face draining of any colour. He could hear Talia breathing quickly, and Stuke was kneeling there, open-mouthed. They waited several minutes, not speaking, almost hoping they would come back. People don't just disappear, after all.

Jalby finally edged forward, straining to see what had happened.

They got to where they'd seen them and found Dorf's navigator, and his torch, smashed on the forest floor. There were broken branches and the signs of a brief struggle. Whatever had happened to them though, had happened very quickly.

Chapter 13

It was a few minutes later when they came across it – a huge steel trapdoor in the ground, surrounded by trees. There seemed to be no way of opening it, and no sign of Dorf and Smoyd.

'Guess we'll just have to keep looking for a way in,' said Jalby.

They wandered on in the same direction and the forest seemed to thin a little. Eventually they could make out what looked like some battlements in the distance. They were on the cliff edge and could hear massive waves crashing on the shore far below.

'Go a bit closer and try jumping up and down,' Talia taunted as Stuke peered over the edge. A small part of the cliff crumbled away and Stuke scrambled back inland.

They reached the battlements a few minutes later. They were solid concrete, from the last century, and looked like no-one had used them in years.

'Didn't you say the tunnels had something to do with the wars?' asked Stuke. 'These look pretty warlike to me.'

'I think the tunnels are right below,' said Talia. 'I just can't see a way in.'

They walked slowly across the top of the concrete, looking for signs they might still be in use. The sound of the water got louder and they could see spray from the waves in the moonlight. It was a sheer drop to the sea, with no way down.

Jalby shivered. 'Wouldn't want to go looking down there. Any ideas?'

'This is hopeless,' said Stuke. 'There's nothing here. I reckon we should head back for the town and come back tomorrow.'

'But what happened to Dorf and Smoyd?' asked Talia. They must have gone through that trap-door. I'm going back to take another look. You coming?'

'Not sure I like the sound of this,' muttered Stuke. 'What if we get swallowed up by the earth as well?'

But Talia was striding off, leaving Jalby and Stuke to examine the concrete bunker.

'Come on, let's follow her. I suppose we should keep together,' said Jalby.

The sound of the waves receded and things seemed calmer as they approached the trees again. Even the wind was now just a gentle breeze. Talia was marching off to where they'd seen the metal door, determined to find a clue. She didn't seem to care that she was making a lot of noise. Twigs cracked beneath her feet, the

144

sound no longer masked by the wind.

Suddenly, Jalby and Stuke heard a different noise. It was the sound of the metal doors opening up near Talia. Their enormous weight was thrust open in a split second by some powerful force. Talia screamed as something started crawling out of the ground. She couldn't move. She just stared as a three metre tall robot sprang from the hole and bounded over to her. Its massive arms grabbed her round her waist and lifted her off the ground as if she was a doll. A second later, the robot leaped back down the hole, taking Talia with it. The doors slammed shut as quickly as they'd opened.

'What shall we do?' asked Stuke desperately.

Just then, there was the sound of another metal door opening up behind them – a door they hadn't noticed.

'Run!' shouted Jalby.

They ran in different directions. Jalby glanced over his shoulder to see another massive robot trying to decide who to go for. Clearly this posed the robot a tricky dilemma, as it looked back and forth.

Jalby kept on running, straight back to the cliff. He realised this was probably not the best decision he'd ever made, especially when he heard the robot's heavy footsteps crashing after him. The robot was gaining and Jalby could see the cliff edge only six metres away. There was nothing he could do. He tried to wrong foot the robot by turning to run along the cliff. The sound of the waves rose up once more. The robot was quick. It was reaching forwards. Jalby felt it trying to grasp his arm. It got hold of his sleeve. There was the sound of his sleeve tearing, and then he slipped. His head banged hard against the cold earth and he could feel himself falling. He was helpless now, tumbling over and over down the cliff – nothing could save him. Just as he thought he was finished, his body came to a crushing halt. It knocked the breath out of him, but he was still alive. He tried to move his fingers. They still worked. Everything seemed to work, but he felt something dripping down his forehead – blood.

He stayed completely still, apart from slowly turning his head to look up the cliff. He thought he saw the robot's outstretched arm, but the rest of it was hidden from view. Then the arm disappeared and he heard the robot stomp back away from the cliff. Clumps of loose earth cascaded down, showering him.

He had been saved by a narrow ledge five metres below the edge. The cliff face looked impossible to climb, but the ledge seemed to stretch some distance into the gloom and disappeared round a jagged piece of rock. He had been lucky – he could easily have fallen all the way down the cliff, or fallen on to something that would have skewered him like a giant cocktail stick.

He lay there for a while. It seemed like ages. He was feeling dazed, but he was starting to get his breath back. The ledge was narrow – less than half a metre across, but he had no choice. He slowly eased himself up and started to crawl slowly, next to the abyss.

The sound of waves crashing on rocks was louder than ever, and the wind was starting to pick up. He cursed as he realised he had lost his night glasses in the fall.

His head throbbed and his eyes refused to focus, but he inched his way forwards. The ledge seemed to be getting narrower, so narrow his left foot slipped off and dangled in the air, a hundred metres above the sea. He pressed himself closer to the rock as he felt the wind whip through his clothing, chilling him to the bone.

He didn't know how he could continue. He wanted to give up. He was losing hope and panic overwhelmed him. His strength was ebbing away when he thought he heard a voice he recognised. He strained to hear above the wind. There it was again.

'I must be imagining it,' Jalby said to himself.

He couldn't believe it. It was Dana.

'Where are you?' Jalby called out in desperation.

It was a moment before he realised her voice was coming from his own head. Was he dreaming it?

'Jalby, it's me, Dana. Keep going. The ledge widens further on. Head for the rock – it will be okay after that.'

'What's going on?'

'It's the zaphalod in the microchip. It means I can see where you're going, through your eyes, and we can communicate – when there is a good signal.'

'That's impossible!' Jalby exclaimed.

'I can help you find me. Then you can help me. Please!'

'Where are you?'

'I'm somewhere in the tunnels under the cliff.'

Jalby struggled on, battling the fierce wind, keeping his body as low as he could. The jagged rock slowly became bigger, but his fingers were numb from holding on. He winced as sharp stones cut into his knee.

'You're nearly there,' said Dana's disembodied voice.

Jalby reached out and grasped the rock. He almost lost his grip, but saved himself from plummeting head first down the cliff face to certain death. He held on for what seemed an eternity, but Dana ordered him on.

'Hurry, there's not much time, you've got to keep moving.'

He hauled himself round the rock and gasped in amazement. There, a hundred metres away, was an enormous cave mouth which disappeared into the cliff.

'That must be it!' thought Jalby.

The ledge became slightly wider and he could crawl along it more easily now. Another five minutes and he would be there. He focussed on the ledge. It was still dangerous. One slip and he would be dead. It was easier to see his predicament – moonlight picked out the spray far below, as massive waves pounded the cliff. Both his legs slipped off in a moment of carelessness and smashed against the rock. Only his hands held him, but his grip was slipping.

'Grab the plant Jalby,' said Dana quickly.

Using his remaining strength, he lunged for a strong-looking root sticking out from the ledge, just as he was about to fall. It was good advice – the root didn't break. From somewhere, he got some strength and hauled himself back on to the ledge. He was sweating, despite the freezing wind.

'Another few metres and you'll be ok,' he heard Dana saying.

He finally reached the end of the ledge, where it opened on to the wide flat entrance to the cave.

The cave was massive. The entrance was at least fifteen metres high. Inside was total blackness and Jalby had the impression it went on for a long way. He collapsed from exhaustion and lay flat on the rock.

'Come on Jalby, you can't stay there,' said Dana, a moment later.

'I thought you said I'd be safe!'

'Not for long Jalby. You don't want them to find you. Really you don't. Enter the cave. Follow it to the end and you'll come to a sealed door. When they brought me here, they brought me through the door in an old cargo scooter. You must do the same, but you'll need to jump in when it passes. Don't let them see you.'

'What will I do when I get inside?' Jalby asked.

It was too late – she had disappeared. Jalby wondered if she had been caught communicating with him. Perhaps they were coming for him. He was on his own.

Chapter 14

Jalby staggered to his feet and looked uneasily into the mouth of the cave. The moonlight barely penetrated inside. He walked slowly forwards and allowed his eyes to adapt. He could just see the cave turn to the right after a while. He kept close in to the side and edged round the wall. The cave seemed endless, twisting and turning into the depths of the cliff. After a final bend, he saw the sealed door, just as Dana had described. The only light came from a security pad at the side. He noticed a camera above the door and hoped he hadn't already been spotted.

Just then, he heard something coming through the tunnel from the direction he'd come. He hid at the side of the cave, making himself as small as possible. A few seconds later, a scooter swept past with several trailers all hovering behind. He risked a glance at the driver - a heavily built man, dressed in dark clothes, with his face obscured.

As the scooter slowed to a halt, Jalby reached over and pulled open the lid of the last trailer. Whatever it was carrying, there still seemed to be space to hide. It was his only chance. Jalby slipped inside and closed the lid as quietly as he could as the man scanned his eyes at the door. A moment later, the door slid open and Jalby heard the driver talking to another man.

'This is the last shipment. It's all there, no need to check,' the driver was saying.

The trailer jolted suddenly as the scooter started off again through the door. Jalby fell against the back with a bang.

'What was that?' asked the second man.

'Just something falling over. No damage.'

'We don't want the boss going mad again. We've already broken some expensive stuff.'

The driver didn't reply, but the ride at the back became a lot smoother.

Jalby guessed they were inside when light seeped in under the edge of the lid. He started to feel more exposed. He somehow had to get out of the trailer without being seen, but when was a good moment? He lifted up the lid slightly and peered out. Rough, rocky walls slipped past. They were going quite quickly. It would be suicidal to jump now. After a few minutes, the scooter slowed down and began to turn. He looked out again. They were going round a bend, and the tunnel was darker here. Now was his chance: the trailer was only moving at walking pace. He could see the broad back of the driver twisting as he negotiated the bend. Jalby opened the lid and jumped out as lightly as he could. His trainers skidded in the dust, but he hardly made a sound. He ran after the trailer and was just in time to close the lid before the driver sped up again and disappeared down the tunnel.

What now? He didn't see any alternative but to follow the scooter. He crept round the bend but there was nothing except the tunnel, disappearing into the distance. He began the long trudge, hoping nothing else would come: this time, there was nowhere to hide.

Soon the tunnel became lighter. He was getting closer to whatever was going on, but there was still no sound from anywhere. He flattened himself against the stone wall and side-stepped round a sharp bend. He was faced with a choice. The tunnel split into three. He took the middle tunnel, thinking it would lead to the centre of the complex. Good choice. He heard a scooter rush out of the right hand tunnel. He went back to the entrance in time to see a boy about his age riding off into the distance.

Jalby hurried onwards. A few seconds later, he heard the familiar sound of more scooters, all heading his way. He was going to be discovered. He glanced round. There was a large pile of junk at the side of the tunnel. He dived behind it, just as three other children flashed past. There seemed to be quite a few children around, and they all seemed to have the same blank, expressionless faces as they stared ahead. None of them spoke.

Jalby got to his feet but then tripped over what looked like an ancient computer – a relic from the twentieth century. Someone was having a major clear-out: mysterious looking tools, broken machines, tangled bits of metal – all sorts of rubbish were stacked against the side of the tunnel. It looked like stuff left over from the cold war, and even earlier in the place's history.

Jalby began to sweat in the heat of the tunnel. He was feeling weak and unsteady on his feet.

'Got to keep going,' he said to himself, as he collided with the wall. He realised he hadn't eaten for hours and swallowed a high-energy tablet he'd kept in his pocket. This would stop him getting hungry for another four hours.

The tunnel opened out into a large room with white walls. It seemed to be a storage depot. Boxes and equipment were lying everywhere, with scooters parked here and there. Jalby watched the scene carefully for a minute before venturing inside. No-one was there. He moved steadily round the edge of the room. Several boxes were open and he peered inside. There were hundreds of scientific looking components: dials, tubes, electronic meters. They could supply a big laboratory, thought Jalby – far bigger than the one back at the institute. Whatever was going on was going to be large scale.

Just then Jalby heard voices coming quickly along a corridor. He hid behind a large packing case with 'Made in China' stamped across it. Two scientists headed for one of the opened boxes, with their white lab coats flowing behind them.

'These memory boards are far better than anything made here,' one of them said.

'Another few days and we'll have ten machines going,' the second scientist said.

'How many have we got so far?'

'Four, including the specially adapted one.'

The men's voices trailed off as they walked back along the corridor.

Jalby didn't move for a while. He waited until everything was still and then crept from behind the packing case. The corridor widened and there were windows in the walls on either side. He was in a dilemma. If he went over to one wall, he'd easily be visible to anyone looking through the other windows. There was nothing else he could do. He slipped over to the left of the corridor, keeping low. He raised his head slightly and peered through a window.

A scientist was looking over a row of dials and meters. It was a programmer. A child lay on a hospital bed by the side. It seemed identical to what had happened to Jalby, but this time Jalby could

155

watch the information being programmed on a large computer monitor. He was captivated by the images flashing across the screen: they didn't seem to resemble anything he'd seen before. He stayed there just a little too long. Suddenly there was a shout from a room behind him.

'Hey! Who are you? Stay there!'

A scientist burst through the door of the room and ran towards Jalby. The scientist reached out to grab him, but Jalby ducked out the way and sprinted towards the end of the corridor. There was a bang as the scientist clumsily crashed into the window Jalby had been looking through.

'Stop! Intruder!' the scientist yelled after he'd picked himself up off the ground.

Jalby easily escaped, but soon the whole laboratory would be after him. He passed another room, screeched to a halt, and then jumped through the door. Inside was another bed, with a very large boy strapped to it. Jalby recognised him immediately – it was Gorzon. Instead of Gorzon's usual defiant face, he now looked petrified. He turned his head slightly and noticed Jalby.

'Please help me,' Gorzon managed to whisper.

Gorzon's head was plugged into another programmer, but he didn't seem happy to be there. His eyes were pleading with Jalby.

Jalby hesitated, but he heard footsteps outside – he had to keep moving. Gorzon looked as if his spirit had been crushed as Jalby ran off and disappeared through another door. Several scientists rushed into Gorzon's lab, glanced at him and then went after Jalby.

The room Jalby had run into was a dead end. The scientists followed and surrounded him. One was wielding a heavy looking metal bar. A nasty grin spread across his face as he saw Jalby's problem. Jalby recognised one of the others – it was Scorpface.

'Now, we don't need to hurt you if you do exactly as we say,' Scorpface said. 'Just come quietly with us, and you'll be safe. You can be with the other children.'

Jalby stepped forward as if to give himself up. The scientists smiled as they moved closer to catch him. One of them reached forward, but Jalby blocked the man's arm and followed through with a sharp jab to his flabby stomach. The scientist cried out and doubled up in pain. Jalby saw the metal bar swinging towards his face. He ducked quickly and heard the bar swoosh overhead. Scorpface looked the weediest of the scientists. Jalby lashed out with his foot and struck Scorpface's shin before racing back through the door into Gorzon's lab. Gorzon looked stunned as Jalby vaulted his bed and ran on. Jalby didn't even spare him a glance. Gorzon would have to wait.

Chapter 15

He ran straight into another scientist outside Gorzon's lab. The man lunged at Jalby, but was amazed to see him somersault backwards and dart off down the corridor. There were more voices. Everyone was closing in. Jalby spotted a narrow tunnel off to his left, saw it was empty and ran down it, just as more people appeared from round the corner. After a few metres, more tunnels went off in different directions. The place was a labyrinth.

Everywhere, he heard people shouting after him, and they were gaining fast. He stood for a moment, deciding which tunnel to take. Voices were coming from one of them. They were not human voices. It was what Jalby had been dreading. A robot came bounding along the tunnel towards him, with a robot dog in front, snapping its vicious mechanical jaws.

Jalby dived down a different tunnel, hoping no-one was coming the other way. He seemed to be lucky – it was empty. The gloomy tunnel started to descend steeply and Jalby had to slow down before he fell. He could hear the robots turn down his tunnel. The robot dog was quickest, and its harsh electronic bark hurt Jalby's ears. He didn't think he stood much chance of escaping.

Suddenly the tunnel turned sharply to the right and he caught sight of something overhead. It looked like an old ventilation shaft. He jumped up and grabbed hold of the metal edge. He pulled himself up until his legs found their footing, just before the robots ran underneath him. Several scientists followed a few seconds later. They were breathing heavily and sounded unfit, their heavy steps echoing down the tunnel.

Jalby pulled himself further up inside the shaft. It levelled off and started to run horizontally above the tunnel below. A thick layer of dirt covered the bottom. The shaft was just big enough for him to crawl through. Soon he was in total darkness. He had no idea where he was going or if he would find his way out, and he was running out of time. He started to feel alone and helpless. He continued crawling through the dusty shaft, coughing in the foul, stagnant air. The shaft was too narrow to turn round.

Suddenly, something stopped his leg. He tried to wrench it forward, but his trousers were snagged on something. He tried again but couldn't free them. He couldn't even get his arm back to help. He was giving up hope when he heard the familiar voice again – Dana.

'Jalby, I think you're near. Keep moving. I can't see where you are now, but I can tell you're getting closer.

'What happened earlier? Why couldn't we talk?' Jalby asked.

'It was getting dangerous. Someone was coming. Then I lost the signal.'

'The signal?'

'From your brain. I didn't know where you'd gone to.'

'I'm stuck. Stuck in an old pipe. I can't move. They're all looking for me. Do you know about Talia and Stuke? They were outside. I think they got Talia.'

'I've heard nothing. They don't tell me anything.'

Jalby thought he heard footsteps below and fell silent.

'Jalby, are you there?' Dana asked.

The footsteps passed underneath, seemed to pause for a moment and then carried on.

'Yes, I'm here. That was close. There was someone below me,' Jalby whispered.

'Be quick. It's not long now,' Dana pleaded.

Jalby tugged again at his leg. This time he felt stronger. There was a tear and a bang as his knee struck the side of the pipe.

'What was that?' Dana asked.

'Nothing, I'm free. I'm going to see where this pipe leads. Not that I've got much choice.'

He struggled on. Soon, a glimmer of light appeared ahead. He started to crawl faster until he was above another opening like the one he'd climbed into. It was above a small room, with old cases strewn everywhere. It didn't seem to be used much. Jalby crawled across the opening in the pipe and lowered his legs down, before dropping quietly to the floor. The door to the room was slightly open. He stepped over to it and looked down a short corridor.

'Dana, do you recognise this? How can I get to you?'

'It looks like the corridor I was brought along. I'm in a room off this corridor Jalby – I'm sure I am!'

Jalby checked the corridor and ran to a door ten metres along it. There was no window. It was a risk, but he could hear robots coming closer. He burst in through the door and closed it as quickly as he could.

'You've made it!' Dana gasped.

She was being held in an old cell, but now she looked happier than Jalby had ever seen her.

'Quickly, get the keys. I think they're in that box over there. The guard will be back any minute.'

Jalby ran over to a small metal box embedded in the wall. He didn't have time to think. He snatched a set of three keys and ran to the cell. He fumbled with the first key. It didn't seem to fit. The second seemed to fit, but didn't open the door.

'Must be the last key,' Jalby mumbled.

'Hurry!' cried Dana.

The key finally worked and the rusty iron door swung open with a screech. Dana ran out, with a broad smile on her face. Jalby sensed something was wrong. Dana's smile quickly turned to a grin.

'You ok, Dana?'

Suddenly she launched herself at Jalby and pushed him backwards into the cell. He tripped over the step, tried to save himself, but fell on the hard, stone floor. Dana slammed the door of the cell closed. It locked automatically.

'Dana, are you mad! What's going on?' Jalby yelled.

'Relax Jalby, there's nothing you can do now. I brought you here. It was my duty.'

'Dana, you've been brainwashed. Snap out of it. I came here to help you!'

'I have not been brainwashed, and I do not need anyone's help,' she said defiantly. 'It was my job to bring you here. You are what's missing from Dolgov's project. He'll be very glad you've arrived.'

162

Jalby looked on helplessly as Dana grinned again and left the room.

Chapter 16

Two of the biggest robots Jalby had ever seen came into the room, followed by a scruffy looking scientist. A robot dog waited in the doorway, its eyes flashing menacingly.

'Shackle him,' the scientist ordered.

One of the robots unlocked the cell and handcuffs sprang out of its arm. Jalby's wrist was clasped before he could even blink.

'Ok, let's move,' the scientist said sternly.

The handcuffs shortened until Jalby was firmly chained to the side of the robot, and off they marched down the corridor.

'Where are we going?' asked Jalby, as boldly as he could.

'You'll have the honour of meeting the boss. We'll be there very shortly,' replied the scientist.

Jalby didn't try to struggle – there was no point. He may as well have fought against a solid rock. He was taken to the end of a long corridor, through a sealed door and into a vast room. Computers hummed away, their banks of lights blinking as scientists scurried around.

'Ah, here he is! Glad you could join us Jalby.' A tall, well spoken scientist turned to face Jalby and strode purposefully across the room towards him. The scientist looked like he had almost been good-looking once, but he was painfully thin and his skin had a sickly colour.

'I am Dolgov. No doubt you've heard of me.'

The man had a nervous twitch whenever he spoke – as if something else was in control of his face.

'Not sure I have, actually,' Jalby lied.

Dolgov ignored Jalby's comment.

'I hope you had a comfortable journey,' he continued. 'I gave Dana a challenge – to see if she could bring you to my laboratory, after my robots failed to catch you. She did an excellent job of leading you here.'

Jalby noticed several large overhead screens. One was switched on and showed Gorzon strapped to the bed in his lab. He seemed to be able to hear and see what was going on in the control room.

'What are you doing to Gorzon?' Jalby asked suspiciously.

Dolgov glanced up at the screen and smiled at Gorzon. Gorzon didn't smile back.

'As you may know, Gorzon could not be programmed,' Dolgov

replied. 'He has a certain condition, which means it cannot work on him.'

'So why is he connected to a brain programmer?'

'That is not a programmer – it is a deprogrammer,' Dolgov laughed loudly. 'It removes things you've learned – anything we select – even memories. In a few more hours, the machine will have carefully removed all the Chinese he has ever learnt. He will no more be able to speak Chinese than you or I can speak Ancient Greek.'

'What's the point of that?' asked Jalby, frowning.

'Where's your imagination?' Dolgov replied. 'Just think. I will be able to remove anything which could affect my plans.'

Jalby remembered what had happened to Gorzon's father – how he had been pushed from the cliffs. 'Gorzon's memory of his dad, for example?' he asked.

'By removing the cause of any trouble, everyone benefits,' Dolgov answered mysteriously. 'But we are getting side-tracked – I was going to tell you about my improvements to brain programming.'

A manic look appeared in the scientist's eyes. Dolgov was enjoying being the centre of attention. It was like watching the teacher's pet explaining how he got the answer in the hardest science question.

'You're going to turn Dana into a slave!' Jalby interrupted.

'I don't like this word "slave",' Dolgov sneered. 'I prefer the phrase "human robot". A slave doesn't like the work he or she is doing – but a human robot won't even think about it.'

Jalby was puzzled. Why would Dolgov set up a whole laboratory if he had only adapted one microchip? It didn't seem very ambitious.

'So you and your human robot are going to rule the world!' Jalby said sarcastically.

'That's not quite correct,' replied Dolgov slowly. 'The zaphalod turns the child's brain into a transmitter. As soon as the child robot is activated, their brain will send out signals turning all other programmed children into robots, wherever they are – including the children I programmed in that quaint little seaside town along the coast. Clever, eh?'

Jalby felt his stomach lurch. 'You mean it will be like a chain reaction?' he asked.

'Exactly!' said Dolgov, looking particularly pleased with himself. 'These human robots will automatically bring even more children to my laboratory to be programmed – children from London, Paris, wherever... Soon, every child you see will have been programmed – and they will all turn immediately into robots – my robots. My programming machines are almost ready to transform your future!'

Dolgov's plan, if true, would mean the end of freedom for children. It was a terrifying thought. Children everywhere would be doing Dolgov's dirty work – whatever that might be.

'Some future!' Jalby said contemptuously.

'Jalby, you children have to do something! You can't expect to be educated and then to sit doing nothing – or playing computer games. What a waste!'

Stuke's approach to life suddenly seemed much more attractive to Jalby. Sitting around and messing with scooters was infinitely preferable to being in a mad scientist's experiment.

'School has become obsolete,' continued the scientist. 'At least I, unlike Professor Meribrayne, am offering you an alternative – something to do with your lives – something to stop you getting bored!' He was about to explode with excitement.

'And just what sort of work are we supposed to be doing?' Jalby asked.

'You will be responsible for keeping adults in line,' Dolgov replied darkly. 'For too long I have played second fiddle to people like Meribrayne. I have always had to follow orders, even though it

168

was me with the ideas. My scientific genius means I don't need to live in a world of mediocrity – not any more!'

'Why can't you use normal robots to control people – like most mad scientists try to do?'

Robots were not the best at answering telephones or dealing sensitively with people, but surely that hardly mattered when you were interested in world domination.

'Robots may be strong Jalby, but they'll never be as intelligent as a well-educated child. It's intelligence that matters – not just brute force. Wouldn't you agree? Or has Meribrayne's programming taught you nothing?'

Jalby stayed silent. He was thinking about how he had made it as far as Dolgov's lab. Perhaps he wouldn't even have got this far without the help of the programming. Perhaps he could still get out of this mess…

'Children are the future,' Dolgov continued, smiling. 'You will be everywhere, keeping an eye on adults, stopping them doing stupid things. I would have to build millions of normal robots for my plan to work. Instead obedient children will help me take control. Children really will inherit the earth!'

'But we will be controlled by you!' Jalby exploded.

'A minor matter. Children are inexperienced – that's why I'm

169

here to give you a hand, with a few instructions from the programming machines. There needs to be some discipline, surely!'

'I'd rather be back at school!'

'Where's your ambition Jalby? Think how much more we can all achieve by working together as a team!'

Dolgov paused, as if wondering how to say something.

'There's just one more thing Jalby. You seem to think that Dana has the modified microchip and that she is about to be activated.'

'Well, isn't she?'

'No, Jalby.'

'Then who has it?'

'You, Jalby. You have very kindly brought me what I need to start the chain reaction. The microchip with the zaphalod is buried in your head.'

Jalby stared at Dolgov. He couldn't speak.

'It was supposed to have been in Dana's brain,' Dolgov continued. 'She seemed very enthusiastic about the whole idea and agreed to be implanted with the zaphalod microchip. Somehow I knew that she was right for the job. She is a misunderstood girl. A perfectionist, and highly ambitious – just like me!'

At that moment, Dana walked into the room, accompanied by a robot dog. She was beaming at Jalby as if he'd just saved the day.

'Unfortunately,' Dolgov continued, 'when Professor Meribrayne implanted the microchips, she got them mixed up. I always thought she had sloppy workmanship!'

Everything was starting to make sense. The five microchips were supposed to be unique to each of the children, but Dana had got Jalby's and he'd got hers – the one which Scorpface had secretly added the zaphalod to.

Jalby remembered that only he had had a problem during the programming - the zaphalod had caused the programmer to blow-up.

'The zaphalod nearly killed me!' he said through gritted teeth.

'But you survived – and the programming still worked,' Dolgov boomed. 'I'm sure you'll be a wonderful substitute Jalby.'

Another overhead screen switched on, showing Talia strapped to a chair. She saw Jalby and tried to hide the despair in her eyes.

'We caught Talia snooping around outside. Of course, she has already been programmed, but we felt she needed restraining until you turn her into a robot.'

Dolgov smiled maliciously at Jalby.

'And then there are these two.'

He switched on another screen to show Gorzon's side-kicks, Dorf and Smoyd, trying to fight against the shackles on their beds.

'Not sure they're really worth programming,' said Dolgov. 'I have the feeling they'll be dysfunctional even afterwards. But as they're here…'

Jalby had to bite his lip to stop himself asking about Stuke. There didn't seem to be any sign of him.

'What's wrong Jalby? Cat got your tongue? You should be proud – proud to be the one who will turn all these children into robots.'

Dolgov nodded to the normal robots guarding the laboratory. They picked Jalby up almost effortlessly and strapped him to a bed. A second later Scorpface walked smartly into the lab. He looked like an executioner with his cold, expressionless eyes.

'About time. We're all set,' said Dolgov.

They quickly attached a helmet to Jalby's head and wired him up to another programmer.

'It'll certainly be something to tell your grand-children Jalby. Just think what they'll say when they hear you were the first fully functional human robot – batteries not necessary!' Dolgov roared with laughter at his own joke, but no-one else joined in.

'Do you expect me to have a family, just so they can carry on your work?' Jalby asked.

'You won't have a choice Jalby! You and all the other human robots will have families willingly. It will never even occur to you not to have a family!'

Scorpface was busy flicking switches on and off, muttering to himself. Jalby remembered his time at Meribrayne's lab – it all seemed horribly familiar.

Finally Scorpface looked up.

'It's all ready Dolgov,' he said.

'Well, Jalby, this is not the end. Think of it as a new beginning!' Dolgov laughed loudly and his twitch became uncontrollable.

Jalby saw a large red button on the console next to the bed. It looked like a nuclear trigger. As soon as Dolgov pressed it, there would be no going back. The world would be changed forever.

'Any last requests or witty comments?' Dolgov asked.

The scientist's index finger hovered just above the button. Jalby tried to think of something - anything to stop Dolgov pressing the button.

'Don't you think you'll get bored?' Jalby blurted out suddenly.

'Bored? Of what?' Dolgov replied.

'Everybody doing everything you say. Robots are not very interesting you know. I'd rather spend my life with normal humans – well, some humans anyway.'

'Jalby, you don't quite seem to understand,' Dolgov smiled patronisingly. 'You'll still be human. You'll just be more obedient than usual!'

At that moment, Dana came closer and spoke to Jalby.

'I think you're being a little unfair,' she said. 'You know that normal robots will never be as good as we will be.'

'Me, unfair?' said Jalby, exasperated. 'Surely you don't believe what he says!'

It seemed as if Dana really had been brainwashed by the scientist.

'Ok, ok!' said Dolgov. 'I think we've wasted enough time.'

Dolgov's finger once again hovered above the red button, as if tormenting Jalby. Jalby looked at the screens one last time. There was Talia and Gorzon, and even Smoyd and Dorf, all looking terrified.

Dolgov's finger moved closer to the button. There was an evil glint in his eye as he smiled at Jalby.

'This is it Jalby. Good luck!'

Jalby took a deep breath as Dolgov pressed the button.

Chapter 17

Dolgov looked confused – nothing seemed to be happening. He pressed the button a second time.

'Scorpface, what's going on? It should be doing something!' Dolgov shouted.

'It was all set up perfectly. I, I don't understand Dolgov,' Scorpface stammered.

Dolgov frantically started pressing buttons, hoping this would somehow solve the problem. Scorpface was looking very uneasy as he scanned the computer screen.

'Someone has hacked into the system. They're destroying the files!' he cried.

'Well stop them! What do I pay you for?' Dolgov yelled.

'It's no use, the hacker has got too far.'

'You mean to tell me that this computer system, that you set up, can't even stop some amateur hacker from destroying my work!?'

'With respect Dolgov, I don't think this is an amateur.'

'Then who is it?

'That's just it. I can't see who it is – they've encrypted their identity.'

This time, Jalby enjoyed seeing the scientists make a mess of things. It felt like a reprieve.

'What are you smiling at Jalby?' asked Dolgov nastily. 'Don't think you've got away with it. We've got more machines!'

Suddenly a scientist shouted out, 'Gorzon's missing!'

They all looked at the screen which had shown Gorzon shackled to a bed, being deprogrammed. The bed was empty.

'Where is he?' yelled Dolgov. 'Who was supposed to be watching him?'

'It was a robot sir,' said a worried looking scientist.

'This is ridiculous! Have even the robots gone on strike? Get down to the lab and find him. Now!'

'Yes sir,' said the scientists in the room, before scurrying towards the door.

'Not all of you!' Dolgov screamed. 'I need some of you to move him to another lab.'

Jalby's face fell.

'Not smiling now, are we Jalby? Scorpface, make sure the new computer works this time. I want no excuses.'

'Yes Dolgov. It will just take a few minutes to set it up.'

'The rest of you, get him off this bed and take him to lab D4.'

Suddenly Dolgov's jaw dropped. He was staring at one of the other screens on the wall.

'What on Earth?'

Everyone followed his gaze and saw a small boy unshackling Talia. It was Stuke.

'What's he doing here? Who let him in? Send the guards - NOW!' bellowed Dolgov.

One of the scientists pressed an alarm and, a few seconds later, several robots stormed into Talia's lab. But Stuke had been too quick. There was no sign of him or Talia.

'Damn!' shouted Dolgov. 'You'll all suffer for this!' Dolgov's twitch was getting even more animated, the angrier he got.

'Well don't just stand there. Get moving with him!'

Scorpface had already disappeared to set up the new programmer, leaving three scientists and two robots to deal with Jalby. They quickly unshackled him and one of the robots seized him roughly by the arm.

178

'Good. Let's get going. These will be your last moments as a free man – I promise you.'

'Whatever you say Dolgov,' replied Jalby.

He was dragged off down a tunnel towards another lab. Suddenly the robot's grip seemed to loosen and it came to a complete stop.

'Keep moving to the lab, robot. What are you doing?' One of the scientists barked. The robot was silent. It was as if it had been switched off. Jalby wrenched his arm away and sprinted down the tunnel. If he could get to Stuke and Talia…

'Get him!' screamed a scientist.

A scientist spun round to block his path. Jalby ran up the curved wall, upside down across the roof of the tunnel, and down the opposite side, leaving the scientist staring in amazement.

A moment later the robot came to life again. Jalby darted blindly down corridors, but the robot was closing, its huge feet clumping along noisily behind him. He was reaching for a door when the familiar metal arm shot forward and grabbed him. He slipped over, hitting the floor heavily. It was no use: the second robot arrived and he was dragged back to a lab, where Scorpface was busily preparing a programmer.

'Get him on the bed. The programmer is nearly ready,' Scorpface ordered the robots.

The other scientists entered, breathing heavily, with beads of sweat trickling down their foreheads.

'What's been going on?' asked Scorpface suspiciously.

'A robot malfunctioned,' one of them said. 'It's all under control.'

Dolgov strode in a second later and everyone fell silent.

'Good. There are to be no mistakes now. Do you understand?' asked Dolgov. The scientists nodded solemnly.

'What have you done with my friends?' asked Jalby, as much to play for time as anything else.

'We are all your friends here, Jalby,' said Dolgov unconvincingly. 'But, if you're referring to Talia and the others, they won't get far, don't worry. They'll be joining you very shortly. Scorpface, is that thing ready yet?'

'Just a few adjustments Dolgov.' The scientist peered at the screen. 'Yes, it's ready.'

Jalby lay there once again, helpless, preparing for what lay ahead – a life of servitude.

'Any viruses?' asked Dolgov

'None at all,' replied Scorpface proudly.

'So, we're back where we started,' said Dolgov. 'All that stands between me and my dream is the red button. I'm going to have fun watching your transformation into a civilised being!'

'If that's your idea of civilisation, we're all doomed,' replied Jalby defiantly.

'No. We were doomed, before I came along. Things are going to be done my way from now on!'

Dolgov reached forward and toyed with the button for a few seconds.

'Having second thoughts, Dolgov?' Jalby asked.

Dolgov looked at him, smiled his evil smile and firmly pressed the button.

'Activation initiated,' said an electronic voice. '10 per cent, 20 per cent, 30 per cent' it counted...

Dolgov bent over to speak to Jalby. 'You still have a few seconds of what you call freedom. Only when it reaches 100 per cent will you notice any changes – but that won't be long...' he roared with laughter.

The activation seemed to be working quickly. At least, it did at first: '70 per cent, 80 per cent, 83 per cent...'

'Scorpface, could you please explain to me why it is slowing down?'

'I'm afraid not sir,' Scorpface murmured.

Dolgov suddenly glared at Jalby.

'It's you Jalby. Stop it now!'

Jalby wasn't aware he was doing anything.

'Stop what?' he asked.

'You're blocking the activation process, with your brain!'

Jalby was willing the programmer to fail, but he couldn't believe it would actually do any good. He tried to ignore everything else now and just concentrated on blocking the machine. It seemed to work. The activation was going more and more slowly.

'Distract him! Can't you see what he's doing?' Dolgov yelled.

The count stopped at 85 per cent. Dolgov stepped over to the programmer and stared at Jalby.

'Don't think you can defeat me with your mind games, little boy!' he growled.

Dana started to whisper in the robot dog's ear. Suddenly, the dog bounded over to Jalby, opened its jaws and bit into his sleeve, only just missing his arm.

'Pull!' Dana yelled.

Jalby felt his sleeve stretch as the dog pulled ferociously. He was having trouble focussing. The count started creeping up again: 87, 88 per cent…

'Good thinking Dana,' Dolgov said.

Jalby tried desperately to ignore the dog, but then it bit into his arm.

'Argh! Argh!' he screamed.

He tried to ignore the pain and the feeling of his blood dripping down his skin.

'Focus, focus,' he said to himself.

The count had reached 95 per cent – he was still slowing the programmer, but he could only hold on for a few more seconds. He had given up hope when there was a bang at the door. Talia, Stuke and Gorzon burst into the lab. Stuke was holding his phone out as if it were a weapon. Suddenly the robots appeared to freeze and switch off.

'Seize them!' Dolgov shouted, pointing at the newcomers as the robots stood there motionless.

The scientists ran at the children. Gorzon head-butted one in the stomach, making him double-up in agony. Another headed for

Stuke, thinking he looked less frightening. Stuke swung round and swept the man's legs from under him, sending him sprawling in a heap on the floor.

'Get up! Stop being so pathetic!' Dolgov boomed.

Talia seemed to be hiding something and keeping out of the way. All of a sudden she lifted up a huge axe and headed for the programmer. Scorpface leaped out the way as she lifted the axe high above her head.

'Where did you get that?' screamed Dolgov.

'Try doing some spring cleaning – it's surprising what you can find,' Talia replied. Jalby remembered the junk he had found in the tunnel. Clearly Dolgov didn't realise his base needed tidying.

'Stop her!' he ordered Scorpface. But the weedy scientist was already cowering behind the bed. Suddenly Dana launched herself at Talia, grabbing the handle of the axe and trying to wrench it from her. They were spinning around, as if in a wild dance. A moment later they crashed against a control panel and the screens in the lab flickered off. The count was still rising – 98 per cent, 99 per cent.

'Let go!' Dana screamed. 'You'll ruin everything!'

'That's exactly what I had in mind,' Talia yelled back, before ripping herself away from Dana and barging her onto the floor.

184

Talia brought the axe down with amazing speed. It was as if she hated the programmer more than anything in the world. There was a smash as the axe sliced through the control panel. Sparks flew everywhere. The count stopped. The display flashed for a second and then went black. It was the end of the machine.

Dolgov saw red. He lunged at Talia after she'd dropped the axe. She elbowed him and he staggered back. Scorpface finally emerged from behind the bed and rushed at Talia, but he hadn't reckoned on one of the robots. Without warning the robot came back to life, but something had gone wrong with its circuitry. Instead of heading for Talia, it went for Scorpface. Its arms were outstretched, as it moved forwards at terrifying speed. A second later, its massive hand had encircled the scientist's puny neck. It looked as if Scorpface wouldn't stand a chance. His eyes were bulging out of their sockets and he slumped to the floor in an untidy heap when the robot finally released its grip. But Scorpface was not dead – a few seconds later he started groaning, before crawling pitifully out of the laboratory.

The robot, though, had already turned its attention to Dolgov and was moving menacingly towards the terrified scientist.

'No! Get them – not me!' Dolgov wailed. In a flash, Dolgov was out the door, running for his life. The robot suddenly fell silent once more, as if it had wanted nothing more than to scare the scientist off.

The other scientists saw no more reason to put up a fight. They scrambled up off the floor and limped away as fast as they could. Only Dana stayed behind.

'You'll regret this! You'll never defeat us!' she snarled, before storming off after Dolgov as if she'd already become a slave to him.

Everyone looked at each other, not quite daring to believe they'd thwarted the scientist.

'Well thanks guys. Nothing like leaving things to the last second!' Jalby said, trying to stop his voice shaking. 'Would anyone mind untying me?'

Chapter 18

'So, any ideas where to try now, Jalby?' asked Talia.

They'd been searching the tunnels for the past hour, hoping to find Professor Meribrayne. Jalby was sure she'd been captured and imprisoned somewhere in the base.

'You don't suppose he's taken her with him do you?' asked Stuke.

'Dolgov was in too much of a rush. He thought the robot was trying to kill him,' replied Jalby.

They'd split up, with Talia and Gorzon searching one area and Jalby and Stuke another, before rejoining back in the main control room.

Talia and Gorzon had returned first. They'd tried their best to destroy as much of the equipment as they could. They'd done a good job – there were mangled machines everywhere.

'How stupid of us,' Jalby said. 'We forgot about the screens – there might be a security camera for keeping watch on her!'

One of the control panels was still intact. He started pressing buttons and switches, hoping for a response. There was nothing.

Jalby looked back at the others. 'If we hadn't smashed everything…' he started saying.

'Sorry. I, I've started to hate all this stuff,' said Gorzon.

They all looked at him. It was the first time he'd ever apologised for anything.

'Well, better to wreck it all, I suppose. No-one will be using this place again in a hurry,' said Jalby.

'Perhaps she isn't being held here. We don't even know if she's alive,' said Talia.

Just then, Stuke walked over a part of the floor that sounded different.

'Did you hear that?' he asked.

They could just make out a large metal panel in the floor. They felt round the edges, but there was nothing to suggest it opened.

'It's probably nothing. Let's keep looking,' said Jalby.

Gorzon leaned against a wall, exhausted. A moment later, there was a whirring sound. Stuke jumped away from the panel. It was slowly sliding open.

'Gorzon, what was that you pressed?' asked Talia excitedly.

'It was a switch, under my hand,' he replied.

Stuke peered down a flight of old stone steps that descended into darkness.

'You first Jalby,' he said.

'As always,' Jalby muttered.

He crept slowly down the steps and the others followed.

'Looks like it goes somewhere,' he whispered back.

They passed through a dimly lit maze of narrow tunnels and passages, hoping they'd find their way back out again. After a few minutes Jalby stopped, turned to the others and put his finger to his lips.

'Can't hear anything,' Stuke whispered.

Without warning a robot lunged at Jalby out of the darkness. Jalby tried to dive out the way, but the robot grabbed him round the head with one of its massive hands. Like the robot dog, this robot also had jaws – very big jaws. They were opening up and about to take a huge chunk out of Jalby's neck.

'Quick, the phone!' screamed Talia.

Stuke was in shock. It was a moment before he realised it was up to him to do something. He raised his phone, pointed it at the robot and pressed a button.

'It's not working!' Stuke shouted.

The robot's sharp steel teeth were about to sink into Jalby's skin.

Suddenly, Gorzon leaped forward. He tore frantically at an exposed tube in the robot's stomach, until it broke free.

The grip round Jalby's head slackened. The robot jerked violently and switched off. Jalby wrenched himself free and managed to stop himself being sick on the ground.

'How did you do that?' he blurted out.

'My father told me a lot about robots – including their weak points. He had a factory – remember?' Gorzon smiled.

'What was that stuff about your phone, Stuke?' Jalby asked.

'I got my phone adapted again, before we left. Thought it might come in handy. It should be able to disable any robot, by sending it a virus - in theory,' Stuke said, a little embarrassed.

A look of understanding flashed across Jalby's face.

'So that's how the robots switched off up there!'

'Yes, but I don't know why that one decided to come back to life. It just went mad!'

'Who adapted it for you?' Jalby asked.

'Same person who hacked into Dolgov's first programmer, when you were strapped to it. My phone locked on and told him which machine was about to turn your head into mush.'

Jalby then remembered how he'd broken into the institute.

'Anton!'

'Exactly. He's been pretty useful.'

'Did he slow down the second programmer, too?'

'No, I couldn't get near it in time. Dolgov was right. Somehow it must have been your brain fighting against being activated.'

They carried on through more tunnels until they came to a locked door.

'What now? I can't see a key anywhere,' Stuke said.

'Check the robot,' said Talia.

'What?'

'The robot probably has the key!'

Gorzon ran back and reappeared a minute later with an old iron key. The door opened noisily on rusty hinges. Inside was a bare room, with a dim light in the corner. A figure lay shackled to an uncomfortable looking bed, under a filthy blanket.

'Professor Meribrayne!' cried Talia.

'About time,' Meribrayne said weakly. 'What have you done with those criminals?'

'Dolgov and Scorpface were scared off by one of their robots,' said Jalby.

'Yes, they seemed in a rush to leave – especially after Scorpface was nearly strangled,' Stuke explained.

Meribrayne looked confused.

'And Dana didn't hang around either,' said Talia.

'Ah, Dana. It's a shame her mind was twisted by Dolgov. I wish there was something I could do for her,' Meribrayne sighed. 'I'm afraid it's not the last we'll hear of them. But I'm very glad you're learning to use your powers.'

'Well, we had some technical help from our friend at school,' Jalby admitted.

Talia was looking worried.

'Professor, do you know about the children in the town?' she asked.

'Yes. Dolgov made a mess of programming them,' Meribrayne replied.

'Didn't he remove their memories?' Jalby asked.

'No, I don't think so – not permanently anyway. The memory loss was a side-effect of his programming, but I think I can reverse it.'

'So you can do something to help!' Talia said excitedly.

'Yes, I'm going to start to track them down. The authorities may never let me program anyone else, but at least I can deprogram these children.'

Just then, Meribrayne spotted Gorzon at the back of the room.

'I see they haven't treated you so well either, Gorzon.'

Gorzon nodded glumly. 'They wiped most of my Chinese.'

'Yes, I'm sorry to hear that,' replied Meribrayne. 'Thankfully your friends got to you before your memories were removed as well.'

Gorzon looked at Jalby and the others and managed a smile.

'By the way, Jalby,' Meribrayne continued, 'you may have realised you're still a danger to society. I'm afraid we'll have to do some laser surgery. We need to destroy the zaphalod in your microchip.'

Jalby frowned. He had had enough of people playing with his

head.

'Don't worry. It's a small operation,' she tried to reassure him. 'It'll just take a few minutes.'

He remembered that the brain programming was only supposed to take a few minutes. Still, it was weird knowing Dana could see through his eyes, and everything he was looking at. Removing the zaphalod would hopefully put a stop to that.

Meribrayne yawned and started to look very tired.

'I think we should get out of here,' said Talia.

'Can I find Smoyd and Dorf first?' asked Gorzon.

'Do you think they've calmed down a bit?' Stuke asked Gorzon.

Gorzon smiled sheepishly.

'I don't think we'll have any trouble with them,' he replied.

'Good, so we just need to get past any stray robots,' said Jalby.

Stuke shot him a worried look.

'You seemed quite good with your phone in the lab, Stuke. Let's hope it works this time,' Jalby smiled. 'You first!'

Chapter 19

It was only two days after they had removed the zaphalod that his aunt broke the news to him.

'I want you to teach me Chinese,' Malinka told him over breakfast.

Jalby almost spat his scrambled eggs out.

'It appears as if this programming has actually worked – incredible though it may seem. I want to put your knowledge of Chinese to good use. It's something I've always wanted to learn Jalby, but I've never had the chance.'

This was the first time his aunt had ever expressed an interest in learning a language.

'But auntie, I've been programmed with Chinese. It doesn't mean I know how to teach it!' Jalby protested.

'Nonsense. If you can speak it, you can teach it. And besides, it will give you something productive to do in your spare time.'

His aunt was clearly serious, but the last thing he wanted to do was to spend his days teaching her Chinese symbols.

'It's such a difficult language, auntie. It would take years!'

'Well, the sooner we get started, the better,' Malinka replied stubbornly.

'But I need to help with the research at the institute,' he argued.

On their way back from the coast, Meribrayne had told Jalby, Talia and Stuke that they would be needed back at the institute a few hours a week. Malinka didn't have to know it wouldn't be a full time job. In fact, Malinka didn't know anything about their trip, or Dolgov and his plans to take over the world. But, she had found out that Scorpface was no longer working at the institute, and was even less enthusiastic about the place after that.

'There can't be much going on there if Meribrayne is getting rid of scientists,' Malinka retorted. 'Besides, haven't I told you?' she asked with a false innocence.

'Told me what?'

'I've had a few words with the school authorities. I'm afraid Meribrayne didn't have a good enough plan for what to do with you all.'

Jalby didn't like where the conversation was heading.

'What do you mean?' he asked uncertainly.

His aunt was smiling brightly – which was never a good sign.

'You're all going back to school next week – where you belong!'

Apart from the scrambled eggs, it had been quite a good morning until his aunt had started to speak. He had arranged to go out on his scooter with Stuke, perhaps heading into town to check out any new games at the arcade. He was looking forward to a relaxed life, with no school in sight.

'But we don't belong at school anymore – what's the point!' he blurted out.

'That's exactly where you belong, Jalby. You're a child. And when you come home, I'll be waiting for my Chinese lesson – before you go anywhere else, and before you go off to help in that laboratory. Is that clear?'

If he had to go to school, he was determined to get out of teaching his aunt.

'If I go to school, I'll have homework. I won't have time to teach you.'

'Of course you'll have time! You've been programmed, so your homework will be easy for you. You'll have it done in five minutes,' she said craftily.

There was no point arguing with his aunt. She had an answer for everything. His plans for an easy life were in ruins.

Malinka went off into the kitchen, whistling cheerily. Uncle Balton strolled into the dining room. He seemed to avoid looking at Jalby.

'Uncle,' Jalby asked quietly, 'do you think it's important to have qualifications before you teach?'

It was worth a try.

'Of course it is,' his uncle replied.

Malinka's face appeared round the doorway.

'But I suppose if you have a perfect knowledge of a subject – say Chinese – then you can always help,' Balton said hurriedly.

Jalby's heart sank. It was no use. His uncle had already been swayed.

Just then, Jalby's phone started ringing. Stuke was on the screen, looking particularly unhappy.

'Jalby, I want to speak to you!'

Clearly Stuke had heard the news.

'Hold on. I'm on my way,' Jalby said, before Stuke could continue.

'Finish your breakfast!' Malinka shouted from the kitchen.

But Jalby was already out the door, heading for his scooter. They only had a few days left before school, and he was going to make the most of it.

Printed in Great
Britain
by Amazon